UNDEAD
INCORPORATED

STEVE HIGGS

BOOKS

The dogs appear less in this book than in any other which, if you are big fan of their antics, may be a disappointment. The sad reason behind it is the loss of one of my two black and tan miniature dachshunds who gave life, reality, and humour to this series. It happened very suddenly, and he was not in any way old for a dachshund, a breed known for living into their twenties.

It is for this reason, that I dedicate this book to Ranger. My delightful, smooshy, daft sausage dog who delighted me enough that I felt confident he would delight the readers too. He became Dozer in this series and will, in some small way, be with me forever because of it.

Vinci Books

vinci-books.com

Published by Vinci Books Ltd in 2025

1

Copyright © Steve Higgs 2020

A CIP catalogue record for this book is available from the British Library.
Paperback ISBN: 9781036708658

The EU GPSR authorised representative is Logos Europe, 9 rue Nicolas Poussion, 17000 La Rochelle, France contact@logoseurope.eu

By Steve Higgs

Blue Moon Investigations

Paranormal Nonsense
The Phantom of Barker Mill
Amanda Harper Paranormal Detective
The Klowns of Kent
Dead Pirates of Cawsand
In the Doodoo with Voodoo
The Witches of East Malling
Crop Circles, Cows and Crazy Aliens
Whispers in the Rigging
Paws of the Yeti
Under a Blue Moon
Night Work
Lord Hale's Monster
Herne Bay Howlers
Undead Incorporated
The Ghoul of Christmas Past
The Sandman
Jailhouse Golem
Sparks in the Darkness
Shadow in the Mine
Ghost Writer
Monsters Everywhere

Mrs Monica Moore

I didn't say anything for a few seconds, sucking on my lips in thought until the coffee machine beeped to let me know it was ready to make coffee.

'You believe your husband has returned from the grave,' I paraphrased Mrs Moore's own words. 'How recently did he die?'

Mrs Moore's complexion had grown pale in the fifteen seconds since she made her startling revelation, and I wondered if she were going to faint. 'I don't feel so good,' she announced, jolting me into action.

Lunging forward, I swept her legs around and onto the chairs. She gasped as I threw her around, surprised to be getting manhandled, but unable to resist as she fought for consciousness. The chairs in the office waiting area were arranged in a row so they formed a sort of couch with gaps. Pushing her top half down so she was prone, I said, 'I need to elevate your legs, Mrs Moore. It will help the blood flow back to your head.'

I got no resistance as I stacked one of the spare chairs to

give me some height. Her feet went on it and I fanned her face with a handy magazine. With her resting comfortably, and the probability that she would recover in under a minute, I made her a tall coffee and dumped several sugars in it.

Lying across three chairs, Mrs Moore found her voice, 'Dean died two months ago. Long enough for me to stop grieving, I suppose. I haven't exactly forgotten him though and now I keep seeing him. Or rather, I think I keep seeing him. One of my friends said he walked past the window when she was in a bakery in Gravesend. She was adamant that it was my Dean.'

Listening intently, I made appropriate sympathetic facial expressions when she looked across at me and murmured, 'I see,' when it felt necessary to show I was paying attention.

'Another of my friends suggested a séance to communicate with him. Abby is quite spiritual like that; her house is full of dreamcatchers, spell weavers, and little dolls which she says contain the memory of her pets.'

This time the comment in my head was, 'Sounds like Abby is bonkers and deluded,' but I kept that to myself. I don't believe in the paranormal. Not one bit. However, or possibly because of it, I am a paranormal investigator. A successful one. My name is Tempest Michaels, and I came to my career by accident – sort of.

I used to be a soldier. I spent a decade and a half in uniform, deploying to various hot spots around the globe, getting shot at, and generally having fun. I left because I felt I had done all there was to do and because the government wanted to reduce the size of the British Forces. They were offering worthwhile financial incentives to those willing to quit early, so I took the money and used it to set myself up for the next part of my life.

I chose to be a private investigator.

And that is where it all went wrong. The local paper messed up my advert, announced me to the world as a paranormal investigator and, though I was angry about it at the time, they did me a big favour. There are three of us all solving cases simultaneously now, and I probably need to find a new reception/admin person.

Anyway, that is how I come to have a woman lying on my chairs telling me about her dead husband. My soon-to-be client, Mrs Moore was an attractive woman of about forty. Thin lines on her face gave me an idea of her age, but if she had children, they hadn't affected her hourglass figure. She was short at less than five and a half feet tall, with curly dark brown hair tamed with clips and pulled into a ponytail that fell to her breastbone.

Having heard enough to get a feel for her plight, I cut to the chase. 'Mrs Moore, what is it that you would like me to do?'

Before she answered, she lifted her head, checked she wasn't going to faint, then used both hands to grasp the chairs and lever herself upright. I moved myself so I wouldn't catch an eyeful of up-skirt action as she swung her legs around awkwardly, then handed her the coffee.

Now upright and sitting in the centre chair of a bank of three, she paused for a moment to make sure the whirlies weren't coming back. 'I would like you to find out what is going on, Mr Michaels. I want you to find his ghost and make sure it is properly laid to rest. I don't know much about this stuff, but I guess he is staying here to protect me from something, or he is tied to the Earth and unable to escape the mortal plane due to something he forgot or didn't get time to do when he was alive. I watched them lower his coffin into the ground in Horsten Cemetery in

Swanley. I identified his body. He is dead, but he is somehow also here and watching me. Can you find out why that is and help him on his way to the next place?'

I was used to hearing nonsense from my clients which meant I was well-practiced at keeping the smile from reaching my face. It seemed that years of fantasy programs on the television, plus books and film, had filled the heads of the population with the idea that ghosts and vampires, pixies, werewolves, and elves are all real. Urban legend has taken over to blur the lines between what a rational brain ought to assume, and a variation where they fill in the blanks with utter gobbledegook.

I asked her a question. 'How did your husband die, Mrs Moore?'

A shuddering sigh escaped her lips at the question. 'It was a car accident. It was really horrible. They had to cut his car open to get him out and they needed me to identify him. There was nothing left of his face though,' she sobbed, the memory still too raw to talk about.

I latched onto her statement instantly. If she really was seeing him, if he had walked past her friend outside a bakery in a nearby town, then the obvious answer is that he is still alive. A faceless corpse ... well, I could see how a distraught person might make an incorrect identification.

Carefully, I asked, 'If you were not able to see his face, how was it that you could be sure it was him?'

She shifted uncomfortably in her seat. 'He was in his car for a start. Dean loved that car. He was a successful businessman. He started a business when he left the army,' that sounded familiar, 'and it went from strength to strength.'

'What did he do?' I asked, giving her an easy question so she could just talk for a bit.

'He ran a team of control systems engineers. It was

quite lucrative work. He always said the industry didn't have enough competent firms to turn to, so he filled a niche in the market and hired in a load of guys. Funny thing is: he didn't know anything about control systems. He just ran the business. He was one of those guys who could talk the talk, if you know what I mean.'

I'd met plenty of people like that, but I steered her back to how she knew the body was that of her husband. 'You were telling me how you were able to make a positive ID.' What I was doing was probing for holes because I expected to find one and then use that to find her 'dead' husband shacked up with his new woman.

'It was his tattoo,' she said, staring at her hands holding the coffee cup tightly on her lap. 'He had a unit tattoo. I always hated it; I was never one for ink on a body, but it proved useful in the end.'

'A unit tattoo,' I repeated.

She nodded, 'Yes. About half a dozen of them got the same one on a drunken day in Kuwait just after the second Gulf War in Iraq. What year was that?'

'2003,' I murmured, my mind drifting to memories I didn't want to remember.

'Yes,' she checked with her own memories. 'Yes, that sounds about right. Well, whenever it was, they were all strangely proud to have the same tattoo, like it somehow bonded them altogether.'

I'd never been tempted myself, but I knew a lot of the guys I served with over the years did the exact same thing; usually after copious amounts of alcohol. Nevertheless, what she was telling me was far from conclusive.

'Mrs Moore, could it not be the case that the man you identified was another man with the same tattoo? That would explain your husband continuing to appear to you

5

now. You said there were five other men with the same tattoo?'

Her head lifted to pierce me with a hard look. 'You think I cannot identify my own husband's body?' Before I could respond, she softened, thankfully. 'Sorry, I'm here to get your help, of course you are going to question me. The tattoo was aged, so it wasn't someone who had recently got one done to match and then stolen my husband's car and the other chaps on his team were all different in shape and size, and ethnicity come to think of it. Barnesy was Nigerian maybe. Could be Kenyan, I'm not really sure. Is it okay to just say he was African?' She was asking me about political correctness, but right or wrong to label him in such a way, it was just the two of us talking and no one could overhear. She continued, 'Bob was Scottish and as white as a milk bottle, plus he had tattoos covering almost every inch of his skin. Ginge was … well, he was ginger, and tiny. I don't think he was much more than five feet tall. Beefy was Fijian, and that only leaves Martin, and he was missing two fingers from his left hand. So, you see, Mr Michaels, there's no chance it was one of the other members of his team.'

I took all that at face value and filed it away for the time being. 'What unit was he with?' I asked, regretting not getting the notebook from my office before we started.

Her reply stopped me dead. 'The Special Ops Squadron.' She said it like it was of no consequence and suddenly a row of nightmares aligned in my head.

The Past Can Haunt You

'Dean Moore,' I repeated because Big Ben instantly questioned what I said. He leaned back in his chair, casting his eyes to the ceiling as he let the information sink in. The name was a blast from the past which neither one of us ever expected to hear again.

We were tucked in my office with the door ajar. Amanda and Jane were with us, the former sitting behind my desk, the latter hovering by the door. I called Big Ben the moment Mrs Moore left the office. I'd taken her on as a client because I knew my own mind wouldn't rest now that I knew this mystery existed, but I did so knowing it was likely to pick at some old scars. With no idea what I might find when I started investigating, it was necessary to tell Big Ben straight away, not spring it on him later.

'I don't understand the significance of what is happening,' said Amanda.

'Nor do I,' echoed Jane. 'The dead person is someone you used to be in the army with?'

Big Ben and I exchanged a glance before I answered. I

was lounging against a wall, picking away at the case with my mind so I had something to focus on. I had to stop that now and face the demons of my past. 'Sort of,' I told the ladies. 'Dean Moore was a senior guy by the time we met him and ten years older than either one of us.'

'Talking to us was mostly beneath him. We were there to do a job, and he didn't want to hear our opinion,' added Big Ben.

'Most of them didn't,' I agreed. Seeing confusion on Amanda's face, I accepted that I had leapt forward and needed to explain things from somewhere near the start. 'You know I was in the Army, right?'

Amanda snorted. 'People who pass you in the street know you were in the army, Tempest. It's the way you hold yourself, the way you move.'

'The way you think there are twenty-four hours in a day and have to list them exactly every time you tell the time,' added Jane. We all took a moment to look at her which made her replay her statement. 'Okay, I guess there are twenty-four hours in a day, but you know what I mean.'

Amanda said, 'You know you never talk about it, right? I mean, not that I have ever grilled you about that time, but you change the subject whenever it comes up.' I hung my head and drew in a deep breath through my nose. 'Were you both in the Special Ops Squadron?' she asked.

I shook my head. 'No, we were with the Special Ops Squadron.'

This time it was Jane and Amanda who exchanged a glance. 'What's the difference?' asked Jane.

Big Ben answered. 'Qualifications. The soldiers in the SOS are drawn from all over the army. They volunteer to undergo rigorous training. The most rigorous training in the world.'

'Other nation's special forces would argue theirs is more rigorous,' I commented. 'But you get the idea. It's pretty tough and very few have the raw genetic makeup and mental ability to complete it.'

Big Ben took over again, 'Those who are successful join the ranks of the SOS and will stay with the Regiment for a period of time.'

'But not forever?' asked Amanda, trying to clarify a point before we moved on.

'Not usually, no,' answered Big Ben. 'Anyway, those chaps are colloquially known as blades, and they are the SOS. However, the SOS have weapons, radios, vehicles, all manner of infrared sights, and other pieces of delicate electronic equipment, and it would take years to train them to be able to service, maintain, and repair it.'

Suddenly understanding, Amanda said, 'And that's where you two come in.'

I nodded. 'It's where we met. I was posted to their unit several months before the deployment to Iraq in 2003. Big Ben arrived when we were out there. They cherry pick from the rest of the army to have who they consider to be the right guys to support them. It's all on a voluntary basis again and we were volunteers.'

'We were with the SOS, but not in the SOS,' Big Ben concluded. 'I fixed the weapons, Tempest fixed the vehicles, we got to go to the same places as the blades, we had to do a lot of the same training and fitness as the blades, but when they went into enemy territory to perform dark ops, we stayed behind.'

'Because you hadn't passed the selection course?' confirmed Jane, getting a nod from both Big Ben and me.

Amanda leaned on the desk. 'Okay. Now we know your

background, what does that now have to do with this case and why are you being all weird about it?'

Was I being weird? I couldn't tell. 'Dean Moore was the leader of one of their squads. Six men who trained and operated together and who deployed into Iraq on several missions as a squad. They were heroes, but right at the end, just before we all came home, a shadow was cast over their activities and an investigation started into war crimes.'

'We were all drawn into it,' said Big Ben from his chair in the corner. 'To this day, I don't know if there was even a case to answer, but a lot of mud got flung and the six men were removed from the unit, never to be seen again. I have no idea what became of them, whether the case was dropped or if they are all still in jail.'

'No one talked about it,' I chipped in. 'It was like a piece of the Squadron's history was erased. When the investigators questioned us, they only asked what we had seen or heard. Had we overheard them talking? What had we seen them doing when they were back at the forward operating base? They wouldn't tell us what they were investigating, but guilty or not, the team vanished. I assumed they were deployed elsewhere in the army; to training schools or into administration roles in a headquarters somewhere.'

'That would have been torture for them,' said Big Ben, his eyes locked on the ceiling as he tipped his chair backward to lean on the wall.

It felt like I had been talking for an age. 'The point is, it feels like a ghost, no pun intended, just walked back into my life. Dean Moore is dead according to his wife. She is content she identified his body. However, he is also not dead because he has been seen in the local area recently, both by Mrs Moore, she thinks, and by at least one of her friends.'

'What does the client want?' Amanda skipped straight to the point.

Thankful to be talking about the case and not about my time in the army, I said, 'She is convinced he is dead and that his ghost is now following her around because it is trapped here. She believes,' I said without smiling, 'that his soul must be trapped on Earth and she needs me to determine what is keeping him here. There was a suggestion that he might have remained to protect her from some unknown threat.'

'Like what?' asked Big Ben.

I shrugged. 'That she didn't say. Not that she was keeping it from me. I got the sense that she was clutching at straws having watched one too many episodes of *Supernatural* or *The Ghost Whisperer*.'

'Ooh, yeah,' said Big Ben. '*The Ghost Whisperer* starring Jennifer Love Hewitt. She has got a massive pair of ...'

'Did you express that you think he might still be alive?' asked Amanda, cutting Big Ben off sharply.

I wasn't sure what to say in reply. 'I quizzed her about why she felt sure the body she identified was her husband and her argument was convincing: his tattoo matched. It was the only one he had, and the one on the body was aged like his would be.'

'They all had them, didn't they?' asked Big Ben. 'A picture of Iraq with the SOS dagger stuck into the Tigris so it bled down over the sand. I remember it. What were the names of the other guys in that team? I've been sitting here racking my brains but could only come up with Ginge, and I don't remember what his real name is.

'You've got the tattoo part right. I need ...' I went to the desk to grab my notebook. I had been trying to remember their names too. It was so long ago, and they were not people we really knew. If Mrs Moore hadn't walked through my door, I might never have remembered any of them; they were tucked away in the corner of my brain locked behind a closed door inside a box where I chose to never look. 'There was a ginger bloke they called Ginge; you got that one already, and I think there was a Scottish chap. Mrs Moore called him Bob, so I will assume he is called Robert something.'

'There was a Fijian on the team, I remember that much,' supplied Big Ben, sitting forward, and bringing his front chair legs back to Earth.

'She called him Beefy.'

'What is with you army guys and the nicknames?' asked Amanda. 'Actually, how come you never had one? Or do I just not want to know what it is?' she added tentatively.

'Tempest wasn't interesting enough to have a nickname,' chuckled Big Ben, who had the best nickname of anyone ever in the history of the army.

I thought about throwing a handy eraser at his head. 'My middle name is Danger. No one thought I needed a nickname as well. Mrs Moore also named a chap called Barnesy, but now we are talking about nicknames I remember there was a chap called Martin.'

'Martin?' Jane screwed up her face. 'That's not much of a nickname.'

'If it's not your actual name, it is. His last name was Kemp.'

Big Ben nodded his head. 'That's right. Martin Kemp.'

Jane's face hadn't changed. 'Who the heck is Martin Kemp? Is he some old actor like Rex Harrison? I met an old chap in West Malling last week whose dog was called Rex Harrison.'

'Martin Kemp was in Spandau Ballet,' I explained

though doing so didn't shed any light on the subject. 'It was a big band in the eighties,' I expanded my explanation a little further, saw her expression failed to change, and gave up. 'Regardless, I'll need to look into what happened to them at some point.'

Amanda asked, 'She has the money to pay for you to investigate? Widows often find themselves out of pocket when the dust settles. Funeral expenses, loss of income from what is often the breadwinner in the house.' Amanda was really asking if I was taking on another lame duck case. I was known for it, to be fair. The business made so much money, I felt guilty about earning it all and found myself taking on cases for people who had problems they might not otherwise escape. Not so this time.

'Her husband had a fat life insurance policy which she cashed in already. She also said he ran a successful control systems business. I think she is sitting pretty from a financial perspective.' Amanda nodded but made no comment. 'What case are you working?' I asked her.

'An old lady in Sheerness thinks she is Dorothy from the Wizard of Oz. She's eighty-three and dresses like Judy Garland. Originally the enquiry was about some flying monkeys. I thought there was a case but now I'm not so sure. I'm going to contact her children because I'm not sure her elevator is still going all the way to the top floor.'

'Then what?'

'Then, I'll drop it. There's another enquiry I'm interested in. Some ladies of negotiable affection want to hire us. They think they have a spooky stalker and obviously they don't want to go to the police.'

Big Ben's forehead was deeply creased as he repeated Amanda's words. 'Ladies of negotiable affection? Do you mean prostitutes?'

Amanda sighed. 'Yes, Ben. It's a more polite way to think of them. Anyway, that's my plan for the day. I need to get going actually.'

Jane knew I was going to ask her next. 'I'm still chasing down the Sandman in my spare time. That's just because I don't think I'll be able to let it go until I find him, but I have a disappearance to investigate.'

Amanda asked, 'Is that the one you told me about last week which you think might lead to a cult?'

Jane nodded. 'That's it. The clients are the parents of twins, both aged twenty-two. They still live, or rather lived, at home, but absconded last week. They left behind a note that they were going to help cure death. I found notebooks in their bedrooms and they're quite macabre. I was about to head back there when you said you wanted to talk to us all.'

There were more cases than we could handle. I said, 'Seems we all have jobs to be doing. I'm going to hit the research and see what I find.'

As the ladies left the office, Big Ben asked, 'What do you need me to do?'

Quinoa Salad

I'd given myself a lie in this morning after the events of the weekend where I'd led a raid against a werewolf biker gang who were trafficking humans. My late start meant breakfast rolled into lunch and thus far, all I'd had to eat today was a tuna sandwich several hours ago. I wanted to get on with the research, but the sun was setting outside, and I couldn't continue to ignore the rumbling coming from my core.

With a shout to confirm Jane didn't want me to pick up anything for her, I left the office to find food. The Blue Moon Investigations office is located in the cobbled High Street of Rochester, an ancient city thirty miles south of London on the original road the Romans built from Dover to what became the capital. Sitting on the river Medway, the town has thrived for centuries. It continues to do so now not least because the High Street contains buildings half a millennium old or more, and because the castle and cathedral are even older. These features, and others, draw in tourists like flies to honey which in turn ensures there are many eateries open for business.

I selected Ye Olde Sandwich Shoppe, which is about as authentic as an Armani suit being sold by a market stall and had only been open six months. They made good food though which included a large range of vegan salads. Not that I was about to go vegan, not while the world contains bacon, but I do like to balance my foods, so I don't eat bread more than once a day at most.

Standing in the queue, and eyeing up the quinoa, whole wheat, multigrain, and pomegranate bowl, I heard a familiar voice behind me. 'Wotcha, Tempest.'

I turned my head to find Frank joining the queue. As I looked at him, someone outside the shop looking in through the window moved away suddenly. I pursed my lips for a half second, then moved swiftly, calling, 'Back in a moment,' over my shoulder as I dashed outside.

Frank hollered, 'I'll hold your place!' but I wasn't interested in such trivia and there was no one behind us anyway. I didn't know that I had seen anything worth further investigation, yet my brain told me I had just been witness to furtive movement.

Outside the shop, the bustle of people going left and right continued unabated, none of them paying me any attention. I wasn't looking at them, though, I was looking for someone who wasn't moving. It's a simple trick: the eye is drawn to movement; stay still and you become almost invisible. Standing still and swivelling slowly on the spot, my eyes tracked all the places a person might find to pause. If there was someone there, they were either better at hiding than I was at finding, or they knew better than to stand still and had continued walking to merge with the crowd of Christmas shoppers. It was that, or I was just paranoid, and the person I saw coincidentally chose to move away when I looked. Sucking my teeth in indecision,

I decided there was nothing to see and went back into the sandwich shop.

'Everything all right?' asked Frank. When I didn't answer straight away and chose to glance outside through the window again. He joked, 'See a ghost?'

Amused by him despite myself, I snorted a laugh. 'You don't know how accurate that might be, Frank.'

'Is that your latest case then? Chasing down another ghost that won't be a ghost after all?'

His question surprised me. 'Frank, you sound like you believe I could be right about all the paranormal nonsense. What happened to you?' Frank Decaux, owner and manager of The Mystery Men bookshop just off Rochester High Street, believed fervently in all things supernatural. What's more, he wanted it to be true. Everything from little green men to the Loch Ness Monster were on his wish list for genuine discovery and his belief had stayed true through all my cases where I proved time and time again that the creature we chased was nothing more than a man in a suit. Apart from the Yeti, that is. That thing almost ate me. Regardless, Frank sounded doubtful for the first time ever.

He gave me a despondent look. 'My faith is feeling a little shaky, Tempest. The Kent League of Demonologists is in disarray after the arrests yesterday. Yet again, the were-wolves turned out to just be men wearing costumes. I don't know what to think anymore. I can't work out what is real.'

I laid a kindly hand on his shoulder, and for the first time ever, I gave him something to cling to. 'Frank, there is more in this world than you or I can explain. Just because I keep revealing the man behind the mask, it doesn't mean I can explain everything. Maybe the day will come when I meet a real gargoyle or find myself confronted by a zombie dinosaur.'

Frank brightened. 'Yeah. Yeah, maybe. I'm not so sure about the zombie dinosaur but gargoyles have plagued Rochester for centuries. Mostly they just feed on the pigeons, but they've been known to snatch people from time to time.'

There he was - the old Frank was back. I didn't believe for one minute that I would ever be proven wrong. Nor did I believe gargoyles were anything but ugly stone carvings, but I liked Frank's craziness; he provided me with someone to bounce ideas off which was like a window into the insane world in which most of my criminals operated.

'How come you're not in the bookshop anyway? Business slow today?' He had an assistant; a minxy little thing called Poison who drew teenage boys in like moths to a flame, but it had always been just the two of them until recently. Last week I popped in to find him, and Poison had a cousin with her; an equally attractive, athletic young lady called Athena.

'I just moved house,' he revealed. 'Well, truthfully, I moved six weeks ago, but I haven't told anyone because the house wasn't really liveable. I've had to have a lot of decorating, electrics, plumbing, and other work done. For the first month, I was collecting water from a handpump in the garden. It's a great place though. I've been looking for somewhere unique for a while.'

He called it unique in a way that encouraged questions. I thought about cruelly showing no interest, but I wanted to know what unique meant for a man who was far from ordinary. 'What did you find?'

Almost bursting with excitement to have someone to tell, he squeaked, 'I bought a folly!'

'A folly? A building designed for its attractiveness rather than its purpose?'

He nodded vigorously, a broad smile creasing his face. 'It's a little run down, and it's bigger than I need, but I can spread out now. I have so many things in storage … well, I did have, they are all being shifted into the house now. I've been supervising the transfer of my different collections but having left Poison and Athena alone for the last few days, I felt I ought to come by to make sure they have everything they need and feel supported.'

'That's great Frank. I'll have to come and have a look once you are settled.'

He chuckled. 'That might be a while. I have a lot of boxes to unpack, and there are still a lot of areas to clean and decorate. It's been empty for years,' he explained. 'Would you believe there was no way to connect to the internet until this morning? The last people moved out before the internet was invented.'

An abandoned folly sounded like exactly the right place for Frank to live in. I could imagine him tenderly caring for the spiders to make sure they made plenty of cobwebs to give the place a spooky vibe.

The queue moved forward, allowing me to approach the counter where a chap sporting a waxed moustache took my order, took my money, and presented me with a cardboard carton of super-healthy salad. Frank placed his order, requesting a roast beef sandwich with extra horseradish. 'Let me know if you need me to help with research,' he called as I bade him goodbye and left the shop.

He was great for research, but not this time. Not with this case. At least not yet. I needed to dig into a squad of special forces soldiers, and I had no idea what I might find.

Research

The sun was already nearly down when I left to get my salad, and it was full dark by the time I made my way back to the office. The High Street was filled with enticing Christmas smells and bright lights. If I continued past the office and turned left at North Gate, I would find myself among the Christmas shoppers in front of the cathedral where a huge Christmas tree was erected each year. The cathedral choir could be found there most evenings, entertaining the crowd, and collecting donations for the aging building.

I didn't join them. I had purpose and drive. There was a case to crack and I needed to get my teeth into it.

Warily spooning the salad into my mouth and hanging my head to the side so I wouldn't drop quinoa onto my keyboard, I ate my food without paying any attention to it. My eyes were drawn to the screen where I had five tabs already open. The first thing for me to delve into was Dean Moore's life. What had he done when he was alive?

I found a website for his firm, called Control Systems

Engineers, but the website had been taken down, leaving a placeholder where it ought to have been. It made it look as if the firm was no longer operating; a surprise if it had been successful. I reached for my notebook – I preferred pen and paper for some things – and made a note to question Mrs Moore about it later. If it were her husband's firm and it was successful, ownership should have passed to her, and she should have kept it going. Why would she not want to do that?

With that question still in my head, I opened the next tab and went to Companies House where I looked at the firm's filing record. All firms must register with Companies House where pertinent information is recorded. I didn't know the origin of the system, but assumed it prevented, or reduced, fraudulent practices. I saw instantly there was another director listed and the good thing about Companies House is that it provides addresses for the directors. Evan Allcorn's address was in Swale, a small village the other side of Plumstead. I could visit him easily enough if I needed to, but I made a note to cross reference and find a phone number later, then thought to call the business line for the firm and see what happened.

The phone number was still listed on their website, but it rang and rang without anyone answering it and without it diverting to a messaging service. Putting that line of enquiry to one side, I focused once again on Dean Moore.

He still had a social media presence even though he was dead and such things show up with the simplest Google search. When his widow said his name just a few hours ago, I remembered it but couldn't picture his face. Now I could see it and it looked familiar. Partly, the familiarity was because the picture I was looking at was almost twenty years old. He was with the squad of men who I remembered. Six highly trained special forces soldiers in a group photograph. It looked to have been taken in Iraq, given the rugged, craggy, sandy backdrop behind them. I remembered it, just as I remembered the early days of fighting as we pushed northwards in the country. In the picture, the first I came across, the men were heavily armed and sporting several days of beard growth. Their eyes had been blacked out, which was a thing that became an in-joke. They hadn't been blacked out after the fact using photoshop in an almost worthless bid at hiding their identities. Rather, the soldiers had taken pieces of black card and stuck them across their eyes so they resembled famous pictures of secret ops troops.

I had done something similar, I recalled, though I couldn't picture where or when. It was a case of youthful exuberance getting the better of me. I doubted the picture still existed.

One member of the team had been tagged in the picture, providing me a name when I hovered my mouse over it. Vince Barnes, otherwise known as Barnesy, was of African descent, and handsome in an athletic way. He looked young in the picture but take most of twenty years off anyone and they will look markedly different. He had to be around thirty at the time it was taken, most of the team were, though I believed Dean Moore was the eldest of them. At the time, he was a colour sergeant. What age would he have been when he died? Somewhere around fifty, perhaps slightly over the fifty mark. I doubted it was a factor, so I pushed on, trying to follow Vince Barnes via social media to see if I could find anyone else. Strangely, he didn't have a social media presence. Not of his own, anyway. Other than the picture he was tagged in, I couldn't find anything. It was odd, but not unheard of. I dismissed it and tried something different, delving into the Squadron's history and their social media profile to see what I could find.

Ninety minutes later and with four pages of notes, I hadn't actually found very much. I had one more name, that of Vince Barnes, and I had one photograph showing the six men as I remembered them. There were hours of work ahead of me, but I had to get home for the dogs. Having stayed at home until after midday, I left them in the house when I might more normally have taken them to the office with me. Now they would be impatiently wondering where I was and why their dinner bowls remained in the cupboard.

My car, a sleek red Porsche with a factory fitted body kit, took a hammering last week and was still in the local Porsche dealership getting fixed. I'd cycled in and was going to do the same to get home. Miserably, it had started to rain outside, but wearing sports gear and a hoody, I wheeled the bike to the back door and prepared to leave. However, balancing the bike so I could fish out my keys to lock the door, a pair of headlights bathed me in light as Big Ben swung into the car park.

He honked the horn in an excited manner and rolled down his window. 'Mission accomplished,' he yelled between beeps.

Rain hitting my face couldn't hide my expression. 'What, already?'

He abandoned the car rather than park it in a space and bounced out to join me in the rain. 'Already? It's been two hours, Tempest. You only sent me to satisfy one woman. I could have squeezed in nine holes of golf and still got the task done in that time.'

I rolled my eyes. 'I did not send you to satisfy a woman. I sent you to ask a question.'

He shrugged. 'Same difference. Once she saw me, there was no way I was getting out of there without taking my clothes off for her. Besides, Elizabeth Clement is a seriously sexy lady.'

'What happened to your once only rule?'

He shrugged again, giving his trapezius muscles a good workout. 'I appear to be failing currently. I'll rally around shortly, don't you worry.'

I waited for him to deliver the news, but he appeared to be waiting for me to speak. 'Ben, I left a deliberate void for you to fill with information.'

I got a grin in response. 'I've just been filling a void, thank you.' Before I could get annoyed and punch him, he finally spilled the beans. 'Elizabeth, the coroner, was good enough to look up the information once she was finished playing cowgirl. Do you know, she does this thing where she ...' I held up my hand to stop him and gave him serious eyes. 'Oh, yeah, right, you don't like to hear about my exploits because it makes you feel vastly inferior.' He shifted his stance and raised an arm to stop my slap as it came for his face. 'Ha! Too slow, amigo,' he laughed.

'Will you just get to the point?' I'd asked him to visit one of the local coroners' team, a woman with whom he'd shared carnal knowledge on more than one occasion already and who expressed a desire to repeat the encounter any time he made himself available. I wanted to know whether there had been an autopsy for Dean Moore and what they might have found.

'There was no autopsy,' he finally revealed. 'Elizabeth said they would never perform one for a fatal road traffic accident unless there was reason to suspect foul play. She looked at the death on the central database. His body came into the morgue directly from the scene of the accident where it was identified by the wife. Personal belongings taken from his clothing and body included a watch which was inscribed by his wife as an anniversary present and his wallet which showed the police at the scene who the driver was. Elizabeth hadn't been involved at any point and said none of the other coroners would have been either.'

It wasn't what I hoped for but was what I expected. For definitive proof, what I wanted to do was have the body exhumed. If Dean Moore faked his own death, testing the body in the coffin would prove it. However, that wasn't something I could easily achieve without a bucket of proof to show it was necessary.

'You want a lift home?' Big Ben asked, backing toward his car again. 'I can put the bike in the back.'

The bike would fit easily into the rear of his giant utility vehicle, so gratefully, that was what I did, avoiding the rain which became a downpour about halfway to my house.

The dogs greeted me at the door as Big Ben's car roared into the distance. Bull and Dozer fell over themselves to get to me until they realised it was raining outside. At that point, both dogs, who had been trying to climb over one another to get to me through the widening gap, reversed direction.

I left the bike to drip on the slate floor of my lobby and got straight to the task of feeding them. My two dogs, a pair of black and tan miniature dachshunds, are not the manliest of hounds, but they suit me, and I love them. They pranced impatiently until I got their food bowls close enough to the floor for them to dive at, then left them to it so I could press the kettle into service.

Amanda was coming over shortly, which was a reason to be excited, and also a reason to make sure the house was tidy. Tackling a case involving a biker gang last week, she had been distant until earlier today when she revealed a former fiancé in a coma due to the very same biker gang. She felt inclined to make up for her distance by getting very much closer, and I intended to let her do exactly that.

We were still in the wonderful throes of early relationship bliss where an evening on the couch invariably lasted less than an hour because we had already transitioned to the bedroom. 'Long may that continue,' said a voice in my trousers, as Mr Wriggly made sure his opinion was known.

I whizzed the vacuum cleaner around the house, tidied the surface of the kitchen counters and made sure the house was generally ready for guests before I ditched my clothing and dove into the shower.

Barking from the dogs drew my attention, the sound loud enough to penetrate the noise of the water striking my skull. I stuck my head out a crack to listen, but they were quiet again.

'Tempest, are you in the shower?' Amanda shouted up my stairs. She'd let herself in.

'Yeah,' I shouted back. 'I won't be a minute.'

'Ha! Don't you go getting out, Mr Michaels. I'm coming to join you. I need you to help me get clean because I'm feeling very dirty.'

Mr Wriggly was instantaneously about as awake as he could get. I didn't get a whole lot of research done.

Sleeping on the Job

I was awoken by Amanda, which ought to have been a delightful experience, but was rather more rough and urgent than I might have otherwise expected. Coming alert, I could hear the dogs going nuts at the end of the landing. With their tiny legs, they were unable to go down the stairs so had to content themselves with barking madly from the top.

'There's someone at the door,' Amanda told me, making it sound like it wasn't the first time she'd said it. As I struggled from the covers and fumbled for clothing, she pointed to my groin. 'You may want to wear something tight unless you plan to scare whoever is there away.'

I begged Mr Wriggly to calm himself, but my girlfriend was naked and sitting up in bed which meant he was going to do his own thing regardless of what I thought. Yet more urgent thumping sped me along as I hopped to the stairs with one foot in my jogging bottoms and fought my way into clothing that would hide my ... condition.

The exterior light was on, illuminating several figures outside. That light was motion sensitive, going out just as I got downstairs and flicked on the interior light. 'Tempest, open up, it's raining,' insisted my mother.

What on Earth was my mother doing outside my house at four in the morning? I didn't waste time asking the question, I got the door open instead. I kept it locked these days, even though I live in a quiet rural community, because there has been more than one unwelcome visitor turn up at my house in the past.

Mum bustled in with a bag in each hand the moment I got the door open. She was swiftly followed by my father, who was trying to stifle a yawn but also had bags and thus nothing with which to cover his mouth. Behind them, was Chief Inspector Quinn.

My parents turning up unexpected and unannounced was one thing; they were kind of known for being a bit odd, but seeing the chief inspector made my eyebrows reach for the sky.

Blocking the door, though I didn't intentionally mean to prevent his access, I said, 'Ian? What have I missed?'

'Where's the gin?' mum shouted through from my living room. 'I need a drink.'

Amanda was halfway down the stairs, coming to join the party, but she froze when she heard her old boss speak. 'There was an incident at your parent's house this evening, Mr Michaels. They wanted to come here so I chose to escort them since it was on the way back to the station.'

'That was good of you, Ian. Would you like to come in? I should like to ask a couple of questions about the nature of the incident, if I may.' We were being deliberately polite with each other because we were not friends. He'd had me arrested several times and I had in turn made him look small whenever I could. I'd also helped him crack a bunch of cases and made him look good, and he'd rescued my backside more than once when I bit off more than I could realistically chew and needed a swarm of police officers to help me out. We'd reached a point where we had begrudging respect for each other.

Amanda had worked under his command and disliked him with intense passion. She chose to not hide from him though, arriving at the bottom of the stairs dressed in a pair of my joggers and a t-shirt pulled from my drawers. She had a dachshund under each arm. 'Good morning, Ian,' she managed cordially.

He dipped his head. 'Miss Harper.'

I closed the door and went through to my kitchen where mother had the cupboards open and glasses on the side. The first gin went down neat. Seeing my face, she growled, 'Where's the tonic then, Tempest? I couldn't find it.'

Wordlessly, I opened the refrigerator and handed her a bottle.

Amanda slipped around me. 'I'll make tea,' she said.

While she filled the kettle and mum poured a more sensible glass of gin, I turned to the chief inspector.

'Your parents suffered a home invasion,' he announced.

'Home invasion!' snapped my mother. 'Is that what we are calling it? There was a ghost, Tempest.' She put her glass down long enough to cross herself. 'And it wasn't the Holy Ghost, you can believe me on that.'

I took my time to absorb her words and shot a look at the chief inspector. 'A ghost?' I asked him.

I got a non-committal look which was probably better than him speaking because he'd most likely say he now understood why there is so much craziness in my life. Taking charge, before mum was sloshed for the rest of the day, I took the gin away. 'Was anything damaged?'

My question was aimed at the chief inspector, who said, 'No.'

'Was entry forced?'

'No.'

'Was anything taken?'

'No.'

Running out of questions, I tried, 'Did they make a threat?'

Mum got in before the chief inspector could speak. 'Yes, it did. It said you should leave the dead to be dead.'

'Any idea what that means, kid?' asked my dad.

I held up a hand to stop him. 'Wait, wait, wait. What exactly did it say? I want the exact words.'

Mum finished her gin and eyed the bottle in my hand jealously. 'It said, "Tell him to leave the dead to be dead." Then it vanished.'

'Vanished?'

Dad nodded. 'She's not wrong, kid. It was there one moment. The next it went poof and was gone.'

Amanda handed me a cup of tea which I thanked her for. 'Okay, I'm going to circle back to the ghost bit. I need a lot more detail about what you saw. First though, why are you here?'

Mum's jaw dropped open. 'Because you didn't answer your phone any one of the fifty-seven times I called it!'

Dad shot a look that told me it was my own fault: I investigate ghosts, mum saw a ghost, it's my problem now.

The chief inspector made a show of putting his hat on and moving to the door. 'I think that will about cover it for this evening. I have a team at the property now looking for fingerprints and evidence to show how they gained entry. They should be finished soon, and it ought to be safe for your parents to return in the morning.'

'Stuff that!' yelled my mother. 'I'm not going back there until Tempest has worked out what was going on and caught the people behind it.'

'I thought it was a ghost,' my father pointed out, taking his life into his own hands as he chose to poke the angry bear.

Mum spun around to wag a finger at him, 'You shut yer mouth, Michael Michaels. Nonsense like this didn't happen until you let him be a paranormal investigator.'

'Let him?' Dad's face was mockingly defensive. 'The boy is in his thirties with a military career behind him, love. He does what he wants without my permission.'

'Oh, rubbish! You should have stopped him joining the army in the first place.'

As their argument raged back and forth, I let Chief Inspector Quinn out. 'You might wish to escape while she isn't paying attention. You say the team will be finished soon?'

'Yes. I should think so. There wasn't much for them to look at. The question to ask is how they got in because your parents have a decent set of locks plus floor bolts and a security chain. According to your mother, the first they knew about it was the apparition standing at the end of their bed.'

'Did you check them for narcotics?' I asked, then seeing his raised eyebrow, added, 'That the intruder might have dispensed. A mild psychotropic in an aerosol form could have caused the hallucination.'

'No,' he admitted. 'No, I did not. That was remiss of me. I shall contact the team and have them come here for swabs.'

I stepped away from the door, heading to my home office as I said, 'No need. I have a kit here.' It was just another one of those things I picked up along the way. A few months back I'd come across a chap who got a kick out of drugging people with a hallucinogenic. He was doing it in Chatham town centre where he would bump into them as if it were an accident and he'd failed to pay attention to where he was going. In that moment, he would scratch their skin with a specially prepared needle. Then he would watch the results as the poor victim went nuts among the shoppers.

I chose to avoid a long conversation with my mother and stuck the swab in her mouth when she drew a breath to insult my father again. She choked and jerked away, but I had the sample of cells from the inside of her cheek already.

Dad was trying to suppress his laughter and had to duck as she swiped at him. I offered him a second swab kit as he danced away from a kick. 'What's this?' he asked.

'Checking for hallucinogens.' My statement caused a fresh eruption of questions, accusations, and insults from my mother, but I handed the chief inspector the two swabs, sealed inside the little tubes they came with, and finally bade him a good day.

I was about as wide awake as I could get but I was going back to bed anyway. To my father, who was the only one I would be able to get any sense from, I said, 'I think we should get a little sleep and pick this up again at breakfast.'

He nodded his assent as mother continued to argue, but I left them behind and nudged Amanda toward the stairs, whispering, 'Escape while you can.'

Presently, the sound of a tortured warthog vibrated through the walls as my mother snored. I could have gone back to sleep, but instead, I used the time to find out something that thoroughly disturbed me.

Dead

'Say that again.'

Amanda was snuggled in next to me, with her head on my belly so she could see the laptop resting on my outstretched legs. We were still in bed, somewhere I was very happy to spend time with my beautiful blonde girlfriend, but while she'd drifted off to sleep for a while, I'd used the time to look deeper into the rest of Dean Moore's team. The next one I tracked down was the Fijian chap, Beefy. Beefy's real name was Semi Batiluna, and I used the term *was* correctly because he died two years ago.

'Dean Moore isn't the only dead member of that team,' I repeated.

Lifting her head slightly to look at the screen when I swivelled it to face her, I pointed to a news article I found while searching for Beefy by his given name. 'Another car accident,' she observed, reading from the page.

'It doesn't say much about it here, other than it was a car accident and he was declared dead at the scene. I wouldn't think it much of a coincidence if I hadn't also found a third member of the team.' I clicked another tab at the bottom of the screen to bring up Andrew 'Martin' Kemp. The screen showed a handsome man, clean shaven and wearing a suit like it was his wedding day or he had just been employed in a prestigious role at a big firm and they needed a shot for the website.

Amanda's eyes skipped across the screen. 'Also killed outright in a car accident. That was four years ago. Survived by wife Emily. Go back to the Fijian.' Obediently, I clicked back to the tab for Beefy where she reread a passage. 'Survived by wife.'

I summed up what we were looking at. 'That's three dead men all from the same unit. All survived by their wives with no children and all killed in car accidents.'

She slumped her head down against my abs again. 'That's quite a lot of coincidence.'

I nodded. 'It feels like it to me.'

'Do you think maybe someone is after them? Killing them off one at a time and working their way up to the guy that was in charge of the team? Who would want to take on a special forces team like that?'

'Who indeed?' It sure wasn't on my to do list. 'I need to track down the wives. I expect them to be scattered around the country. Beefy was living in Wolverhampton when he died, and Andrew Kemp is from Newcastle. I know Bob is Scottish ... that's a lot of territory to cover if I have to visit them all, but perhaps I will be able to speak with them on the phone.' I was at the start of what felt like a big investigation, and I knew next to nothing about any of it. The rest of my day would be spent digging into Dean Moore's life as I pieced together what might have happened to his business. I found it suspicious that his wife claimed it to be successful, yet it was no longer operating. When or if I got anywhere with that, I needed to identify the rest of the team. Mrs Moore didn't remember their names, not beyond the nicknames she already gave me. I'd pressed her to remember more than that in our original conversation because I needed to identify them and see if the remaining three were dead or alive. I had a nasty feeling it was going to be the former and I had no idea what that meant.

Amanda and I snuggled for a short while and listened to my mother sucking the plaster from the ceiling in the guest bedroom. They'd suffered a traumatic experience, and there was no way to tell how they would react to it. I would quiz them over breakfast this morning and hope to get a little more sense from them this time. Mum claimed it was a ghost and dad backed her up which left me questioning what they might have seen. Someone broke into the house I grew up in and scared my parents. The message, "leave the dead to be dead" had to be linked to this case, but how had that happened so quickly? With a gentle kiss to the crown of her head, I moved Amanda off me before slipping from the bed. It was time to get up and get going. With a swift message to tell Jane what had happened and that I wouldn't be in first thing, I left the bedroom, and got the day started.

Amanda joined me downstairs thirty minutes later, by which time I had walked the dogs and returned home to find a note pinned to the outside of my door. I had calmed down, sort of, by the time she found me.

Walking into the kitchen, dressed for work, and looking both confident and powerful, she froze when she saw me. 'Wow, I can feel the tension radiating off you, Tempest. What did I miss?'

I showed her the note. 'This was on the outside of my door. I thought maybe it was from a neighbour, but it's from them.'

'Them who?' she asked, unfolding the note. I let her read it, watching her eyebrows lift as her eyes flitted across the page. She looked up at me and back down at the note which she then read aloud. 'It's not safe for them at your house either, Tempest. Leave the dead to be dead. You have been warned.'

Keeping my frustrated rage in check by gripping the back of a bar stool, I unclenched my teeth. 'They know who I am, and they know what I have been hired to investigate. Not only that, they think they know me well enough to judge that coming at me or threatening me is likely to be counterproductive: I'd just go after them all the harder. So, they went after my parents because they're a softer target. Last night was meant to scare them so that I would pay attention. The note is to drive home that they know all about me and can anticipate my moves.'

Amanda looked worried when she asked, 'What are you going to do?'

I let go a deep breath I didn't know I'd been holding and forced my muscles to relax. 'I'm going to do something unexpected.'

Surprise!

The door opened to reveal Big Ben wearing a pair of flannel jogging bottoms and nothing else. He may have been wearing some underwear beneath but generally joked that the industry was yet to make a pair strong enough to take on the job of keeping his meat and two veg in place.

The Dachshunds shot between his legs, running like maniacs to explore and find any food there might be to find before the other got there first.

I fixed a big grin on my face. 'Surprise!'

Big Ben looked a little bewildered, staring out of his front door at me and my parents. We all had bags and there was a pile of bits still in my parents' car to come up. 'Um, hi, folks,' he mumbled. 'What's going on?'

With my grin fixed firmly in place, I started forward, the bulk of my bags and determined gait causing him to step back to let me in. 'We're moving in,' I told him. 'Isn't that great?' Then as my parents shuffled inside with their bags, I dropped my voice to a whisper, 'It's only temporary, buddy. I'll explain shortly.'

He nodded his head around a yawn and patted me on the shoulder. 'It would have to be pretty serious for you to consider moving in with me.'

Big Ben lives in a penthouse suite overlooking the river Medway as it winds its way through the centre of Maidstone. Maidstone is hardly a sprawling metropolis but it's what we call home. His suite sits inside a gated community with security guards to control entry and exit. They don't perform roving patrols, and they are not armed, but it provided an additional level of security that would make my parents feel safer. It also had stunning views from the balcony and plenty of space which included four double bedrooms. I knew he only occupied one but bought the place fully furnished so all the bedrooms had beds and were ready to go.

'Oh, this is lovely!' gushed my mother, dumping her bags as she reached the central open-plan area. In it, a large kitchen backed against one wall with a large dining table and breakfast bar. To the right were an arrangement of sofas and chairs around a huge screen television. 'Benjamin, I had no idea you lived in such a nice place. I always thought a flat would be a stuffy place with too little room to move.'

'It's not a flat, mum,' I pointed out as she continued to look around. 'It's a penthouse suite.'

'Does it come with coffee?' Dad asked. I'd let them sleep in since they got little sleep last night, but when I roused them, I got them moving straight away and dad wanted some wake-up juice.

Big Ben chuckled as he made his way to the kitchen area. 'You like a dark roast?'

My mother has an annoying habit of being critical

when there is no need to be and likes to find fault with anything she hasn't done herself, or recommended herself, or previously approved of. It came as no shock to me when she said, 'It's too big for one person, Benjamin. You need a wife and children in here.'

Big Ben physically shuddered at the suggestion of a wife. He was the type of guy who saw a relationship as an anchor to drag around. Presenting his argument, he clapped his hands loudly. 'Ladies, time to leave.'

I sniggered at my mother's curious expression and watched as she looked around the room to see who he might be talking to. Knowing his habits, I focused my eyes on his bedroom door, from which, a few moments later, three women emerged.

Mum's eyes were as wide as pizza pans. One lady had on a power business suit and a pair of heels with a red sole which must have cost a week's wages for some people. She looked keen to get to work. The next wore sports clothes but had a firefighter's uniform hung over her right arm and a pair of heavy boots in the left. Last to emerge, and yawning furiously as she trudged after the first two, was a lady still wearing her underwear. Her pile of clothing was clutched to her chest, hiding her ample boobs which hadn't yet found their way into a bra. My dad seemed to like her the most which drew a glare from my mother.

Big Ben crossed the space to kiss each of them goodbye as they left his apartment. Words were exchanged at a volume we couldn't hear, but once the door was closed again, he clapped his hands and said, 'Right, who's for coffee?'

He got a disapproving look from my mother. 'What were you doing with those poor women?'

'Providing a service,' he answered jovially. 'This place is big, but there is rarely only one person here.'

Pursing her lips tightly, mum decided. 'I can't stay here, Michael. Take me home.'

'It's not safe there, love,' he argued.

I agreed with him. 'That's right, mum. This is your safe place. It won't be for very long.'

'How long?' she snapped out the obvious and unknowable question.

Big Ben went back to the coffee machine. 'Okay, someone ought to tell me what is going on.' He had a right to know why we were invading his house early on a Tuesday morning so I told him all about the 'ghost' who woke my parents, then handed over to dad so he could provide a better description than I got last night.

'It was a pale light,' he tried to explain.

'No, it wasn't, you daft old fool,' railed my mother in response. 'It was a skeletal figure wearing a cloak.'

'A cloak?' dad questioned. 'How much wine did you have last night? There was no cloak.'

I held up my hand. If they had been hit with a hallucinogen, this was exactly what I would expect – completely different versions of the same event as each was entirely concocted in their separate minds. 'That will about do for ghost descriptions.' I moved past it, telling Big Ben about the threats, about the note on my door and what I had already found out about Dean Moore's team.

'I have no idea what that all means yet, buddy, but we need to work this out quickly because someone is quite definite that they do not want me looking at this case.' Then I told him about the person watching me at the sandwich shop.

'They've been onto you from the start then,' he

observed as he served my parents breakfast; avocado on toast with poached eggs which he expertly made while they watched.

I didn't like it, but I had to agree. 'Whoever they are, yes. It seems likely Mrs Moore is being tailed. The question is why.'

Body Count

I left my parents at Big Ben's place with a plea that they stay there for the day. They had all the provisions they would need, plus books to read, a television with DVD library, and mum had her knitting bag which went everywhere with her. They could walk the dogs around inside the fence line and were as safe as I could make them for now.

Big Ben drove me to the office, but I had quite a list of things to do already. It started with identifying the rest of the team and finding them if I could. Thankfully, my colleagues at the business saw fit to help me out.

'I found Edgar Salter,' announced Jane the moment she saw me. She was working out of what had originally been designated as my office. The building came with two built in offices. When we moved in, Amanda and I had taken one each which left Jane, who at the time was the office assistant, at a desk close to the doors to field customers dropping in. That didn't work once she started taking her own clients, so now we hot desk whichever desk is free, and it works ninety percent of the time.

42

I said, 'Cool, where is he?'

'Not too far away, actually,' she was focused on the screen in front of her face but pushed away now to look up and see that I wasn't alone. 'Oh, hi, Ben,' she chucked him a wave. 'Edgar married a woman from Hastings and went to live just along the coast in Rye. He's still there, but before you rush off to quiz him, there's a catch.'

I stopped moving. 'He's dead, isn't he.'

Jane nodded her head slowly. 'He was killed in a car accident on July 8th of last year.'

Another car accident.

Amanda emerged from the other office. 'There's no chance it is a coincidence now. That's four of the team to be killed in the same way.'

Inside my head, my brain began to race. Whoever was behind this didn't want me to look because they knew I would find something, and I already had. There was a conspiracy to kill the members of a special forces team, a team who had been disgraced by something they allegedly did in Iraq years ago. To add to the list of things I wanted to know, I now felt I needed to dig into what might have happened, or what it was they were accused of and that was going to be a harder detail to uncover.

I took a slow breath, in and out, then took a mental leap, 'I think the last two men have to be my primary focus. Four out of six are dead. I don't know what their big secret is, or what might have caused this to happen so long after the events in Iraq. It might be that the events there are not related to this, but I'm not stopping until I track down the last two men.'

'Do you even know their names?' asked Amanda, making a pertinent point.

'Vince Barnes and Bob. Vince Barnes appears in a

photograph on Dean Moore's social media, but that was all I found. I need to know where he is now. I'm going back on social media to find old members of the Squadron. They will be remembered by someone. We just need to cast the net wide enough.'

Big Ben volunteered. 'I can tackle that.'

'Then I need to visit Mrs Moore again. I think the face-to-face approach will work nicely.' I didn't get the impression that Mrs Moore had been hiding anything from me, but her husband's business had flatlined at some point and I wanted to know why. Then I remembered the other director; the one named on Companies House. I'd been all over it and ready to pursue the case yesterday evening. Then Amanda arrived and took off her clothes. After that, everything else seemed too trivial to think about.

Since Jane was still sitting at the desk and operating the computer, which took me back to when she started and the exciting days of having an assistant for the first time, I asked her to find the number I needed.

'That shouldn't take me long,' she said. 'Do you want me to get on that now, or finish what I'm doing first?'

'When you get to it, please. I have a mountain of rocks to look under and no idea which one of them might yield a piece of worthwhile information.' I took out my phone, intending to call Mrs Moore, when it began to ring in my hand.

The number displayed on the screen wasn't one I knew. 'Good morning. This is Tempest Michaels of the Blue Moon Investigation Agency; how may I help you?'

'There's a monster in my closet!' a man blurted, beginning to speak before I had even finished my introduction. He sounded elderly, the wobble in his voice reminding me of my own grandfathers' before they passed.

This wasn't the first time I'd received a call from a desperately panicked person. 'Monsters in closets is our speciality. Can I take your name, please?'

A sob escaped before he said, 'My children think I've gone senile. They want to put me in a home, but there's nothing wrong with my brain. I've got something living in my closet and it keeps trying to get out. I've moved room twice, but it follows me wherever I go.'

'Yes, I understand, Mr ...'

'Best. Ramone Best. Can you come today?' he really sounded desperate. 'I need to get some sleep, and the monster won't let me!' he wailed the last sentence like a person at their wits end.

I grimaced for I didn't want to go. I didn't want to be distracted from the task at hand, but I also didn't want to say no to the poor man at the other end; being a soft touch for people in need has rarely done me any good but we cannot change what we are.

'I need an address, sir.'

'Can you come today?' he repeated, the tremor of hope in his voice made my heart want to break.

Big Ben frowned at me. He couldn't hear what the other person was saying but he was close enough to pick up on the tone of my words. 'That depends on where you are, sir. I have a full schedule already today but tell me where you are, and I shall see what I can do.' Monster in a closet was a new one on me despite my earlier statement. I had a feeling this was going to be easy enough to fix though.

He gave me his address. 'That's less than ten minutes from where I am, Mr Best. I'll see you shortly. You may wish to put the kettle on.'

'Really? You're coming now?'

I shot my cuff to check the time: 1017hrs. I had plenty

to do, but I could delay speaking to Mrs Moore for half an hour.

As I ended the call, Big Ben was still looking at me expectantly. 'Can I borrow your wheels?' I asked.

He started toward the door. 'I'll drive. This sounds more interesting than looking for two men who might not want to be found.'

'I'll find them,' shouted Jane from my office and I waved her a thank you on my way to the door. It was rescue time.

There's a Monster in my Closet

Mr Ramone Best lived in Strood, a town within the city of Rochester which sat on the other side of the river Medway. The office was close enough that I could smell the river from it most days so despite roadworks and traffic, it only took us nine minutes in the car to find his house.

He was waiting at the window, the curtain falling back into place once he saw us get out of the car and head his way. His house was set well back from the road to match all the houses around him because he lived in a large, detached house at the top end of Watling Street. Backing onto open countryside, the area was known for being the most expensive postcode in Strood which instantly made me question if that was the motivation behind the attacks. I labelled them as attacks because scaring an old man alone in his house is a frightfully cowardly thing to do.

The large oak door opened before we got to it, a frail man in his late eighties appearing from the gloom inside to greet us. His breath formed a cloud of vapour above his head, reminding me how cold it was today. He stepped outside into the daylight, a walking stick in his left hand to help keep him steady. He had only a few wispy white hairs on his scalp and a few days of white stubble on his face that made him look a little scruffy. However, there was a sense of style about the man evident in the deep blue paisley smoking jacket he wore over his clothes, and a polka dot red on white bow tie around his neck.

'Good morning, Mr Best, thank you for calling us.' I put out my hand for him to shake.

'You're thanking me? I think you have that about face, young man. Please, come in.' Then he spotted Big Ben lumbering along behind me. 'Goodness, did he fall into some magic potion as a child? He's enormous.'

'That's what she said,' chuckled Big Ben, but the comment went right over the old man's head.

Inside, the house was an impressive place. Wood panelling lined the walls to waist height where expensive wallpaper took over. The ceilings were all higher than one would find in a standard house and the décor was in prime condition as if it had just been finished. My phone beeped with an incoming message. A quick glance revealed it was Jane supplying the phone number for Evan Allcorn. I put the phone away again because I was going to deal with Mr Best's issue first.

Ramone led us through his house. 'You said to put the kettle on. I wasn't sure if you were joking or not, but I have a fresh pot of tea brewing if you are interested. It's so rare that I get to talk to anyone new.'

Big Ben rubbed his hands together. 'A cup of tea sounds perfect.'

At a table in his kitchen, we discussed the subject of my fee, dispensed with the formality of paperwork and I got down to it. 'I need to see the closet, Mr Best.'

'Righto.' He wobbled back to his feet.

'Perhaps you can give us directions,' I suggested.

He nodded and sat down again. 'Yes, that may be better. I'm not as fast as I used to be. It's more than one closet you need to look at though.'

Five minutes later, Big Ben and I returned downstairs to find my client dunking a biscuit in his tea. Onto the table I ditched the device we found. 'Someone has been getting handy with a little DIY,' I explained as he stared at the battery-operated popper. 'This is what has been making the closet door open.'

It was a small plastic box, barely bigger than my thumb, that contained a simple solenoid and actuator rod. Press a button to activate the solenoid and the rod pops out. It probably had a dozen different uses in different devices but here it was being used to frighten an old man. I showed him how it ought to work, but because I didn't have the remote for it, I couldn't make the rod pop and had to give a lengthy description with actions.

'That's it?' Ramone asked. 'I feel so silly now. All this fuss because of a little trick. I should have been able to find that myself.'

'It wasn't easy to spot,' Big Ben assured him. 'It was right up in the top corner of the door. I only saw it because it's eye height for me.'

'And we knew to look for something like it,' I added. 'These are fitted to every closet in your house. My guess is the perpetrator fitted the first one and when it worked, he or she then fitted more of them when they discovered you tried moving rooms. The question I need you to answer is who has been coming and going from your house? Who has access and could have done this?'

The soggy end of Ramone's biscuit lost is structural

integrity and plopped into the cup with a splash. He said a rude word. 'Don't you just hate when that happens?' Sniffing deeply, he said, 'The answer to your question is that a lot of people have been back and forth over the last few months. My two children, who have been hinting at my growing decrepitude for years, changed their tune and chose to pay to have the house redecorated. Most of what you see is relatively new. They are getting it ready for sale.' Seeing the look on my face, he said, 'I'm not daft. I let them do it because I have no intention of letting them sell, letting them push me out of here and into a home, or of popping my clogs any time soon.'

'But you suspect them?' I sought to clarify.

He tutted. 'One never likes to think ill of one's own children, but they are not the nicest pair. The house next door went for two million pounds five years ago. I foolishly let that slip in conversation one day and they have been quietly gunning for me to give them the house ever since. I'm tempted to leave it to the Dog's Trust or someone like that. I expect there's plenty of charities more worthy than my children.' He paused for a moment, moving his upper row of dentures about as he thought. 'To answer your question, yes, I suspect my children. It could be either or both, my money is on the latter. They always did like to scheme as kids. Can you prove it?'

I lowered myself into the chair opposite and picked up the device again. 'Are you on social media?'

Ponytail

Ramone was not only on social media; he was like a rash on the internet. What we didn't know was that the man was a bestselling novelist with a huge following. Using that, we set a fun little trap for whoever was behind the monster-in-the-closet trick and went on our way. We could probably lift a print from the device if we chose to and would try if it proved necessary. Catching them red-handed sounded better and would yield a more conclusive result, plus I had no easy way to get a fingerprint from either of his children to which I could match what I found on the device.

If it turned out the culprit was one or both of his children, Mr Best could decide whether to press charges or not.

The lure set, and the client feeling vastly relieved, Big Ben and I pushed onwards. From the car on our way to Mrs Moore's house, I called the number Jane found for Evan Allcorn. The phone rang and rang and went to voicemail. I debated leaving a message but elected to try again in a short while.

Now that my phone conversation was aborted, Big Ben

asked what I proposed to do about Mr Best's closet monster. I tried to fight the broad grin as it spread across my face, but I just couldn't – I'm a big fan of irony. 'I think we give them what they least expect.'

'Tonight?'

'That depends on whether Mr Best gets back to us. Are you free?'

It was his turn to grin. 'I am for that. It sounds like fun.' It wasn't the first time we'd pulled a stunt like this; they always went well and gave us something fun to talk about at the pub on a Friday night. Tales of the ilk were what made the rest of the chaps want to join in.

Mrs Moore's house in Swanley wasn't far from where her husband had allegedly been sighted by a friend. That she was adamant he was dead and laid out the facts in a convincing way bothered me. My gut reaction was to assume he was not dead, if indeed he had been seen. But the alternative theory, if I assume that he is dead, is that her friend, and indeed Mrs Moore herself, had seen someone that looks similar to her husband. The concept of a doppelganger wasn't beyond belief, every public figure on the planet has doubles making money just because they look like a film star or a politician. None of those assumptions addressed the fact that three more of his team died the same way, and that someone left a threat on my door this morning.

I thought of Swanley as a rundown town where no one nice lived and nothing nice existed. It was a biased impression with no founding, which proved true when we drove into the streets near to Mrs Moore's address.

Big Ben whistled appreciatively. 'You said her husband started a control systems company when he left the army?'

'That's right. She said he did rather well at it, and that's why we are here. One of the reasons, anyway,' I corrected myself. 'The firm appears to no longer exist and that confuses me. That's why I want to talk to his business partner.' I tried Evan's phone again and got the same result. I didn't leave a message this time either.

Passing large, detached houses as we cruised through suburban Kent, a left turn brought us onto her street. The Satnav in Big Ben's car delivered us to her address where an electronic gate barred our entry. He buzzed down his window to use the intercom, letting the frigid air outside sweep in.

'Hello?' I recognised her voice when she spoke.

Big Ben ought to have let me speak, but he's way too much of a dickhead for that. 'Hey, babe,' he purred. 'Big Ben is here; you can relax now. Why don't you let me in, little pig? Trust me when I say you'll want me to save all my huff and puff for you.'

A beat of silence passed, then the gate began to slide open. He turned his head in a deliberately slow fashion to show me his cat-like grin. Mercifully, she ruined his moment by saying, 'Sorry, I couldn't hear you properly. I think the intercom must be playing up. Please, come in.'

Much like Ramone Best, Monica Moore came to the door to find us. She had a fitted dress which seemed out of place to be wearing around the house, yet completely in keeping with her opulent surroundings. Seeing me walk around the front of Big Ben's car, she said, 'Oh. I thought it was the plumbers arriving.'

'I can be your plumber,' Big Ben growled playfully. Mrs Moore eyed him sceptically and I got in quickly before the oversized, oversexed doofus could say anything else.

'Good afternoon, Mrs Moore. This is my colleague, Benjamin Winters. He suffers from an abundance of stupidity. I need to ask you some more questions to do with your case. May we come inside?'

'Of course. Please.' She turned and went back into her house which meant she missed Big Ben kicking my foot to make me stumble when I followed her. I had to grab the doorframe to stop myself from landing on her. I shot him a warning look which only encouraged him to play the clown a little more. We badly needed someone to start shooting at us just so he would start taking things seriously.

He bowed at the door so I could go first. 'After you, Brother Weasel,' he smirked, reminding me of a recent honorary name I'd been given by a biker gang. I got called Weasel while he was named Sasquatch, and I had to wonder if ribbing me about it would ever get old.

'What is it you want to know, Mr Michaels?' she asked as she led us through her wide marble-floored lobby to an anteroom.

'Is this a new place you've just moved into?' I asked, changing my intended question to one which had just occurred because there were packing boxes stacked in one corner.

Her eyebrows raised as if the question were impertinent to ask, but said, 'No. I want to move though. This place has too many memories attached to it. I always feel that Dean is in the next room or just about to walk through the door. I have money now; his life insurance pay-out was quite generous, and I sold his firm as well. I doubt I got full value for it, but it was enough for me to never think about money again.'

Her answer sounded honest; she had money and never had to work again. Not everyone would admit to that. 'Your husband's firm is something I wanted to ask you about. You say you sold it. Who did you sell it to?' I didn't ask if she was aware that they had ceased trading, holding that question back for now.

Once again, I got an open and honest answer. 'To his former business partner, Evan Allcorn. He snapped my arm off when I accepted his first bid. We spoke the day Dean died. No, wait.' She took a moment to think about her statement. 'No, I think it was the day after. He didn't know about Dean, I had to break the news to him. He was the brains behind it, you see. He was the one who knew control systems. They first met by accident at Tonbridge golf club about five years ago. There was no suggestion they would ever go into business together, but I knew Dean hated the job he found himself doing. He hated working for other people. He said he could never earn his worth that way, he would just be a slave making other people rich. Anyway, they met again about a year ago and got to talking. The next thing I knew, Dean borrowed some money to get the firm started, and it quickly went from strength to strength. Soon they were turning work away; that's how it seemed to me. Dean ran the office side of things, did the bookkeeping, hiring equipment, arranging the diary et cetera. Evan ran the crews and got the work done.

The sound of breaking glass stopped the conversation sharply and I snapped my head around to look back at the front of the house. Neither Big Ben nor I moved for a second, rotating our heads back to look at Mrs Moore again. Her cheeks were flushed bright red with embarrassment; she knew what this was, but when we heard another window being smashed, we left her and started running.

As we neared the front of the house and sprinted flat out across the marble lobby, a voice rang out from outside. 'Did you think we wouldn't find you, Monica?' They knew her name, so they weren't here by accident. Was this the same people who left the note at my house and threatened my parents? Was I about to burst through the door and find Barnesy or Bob, the two yet to be located members of Dean's team?

The door opened inward, just like all front doors, and that slowed us down, but not for long as I bounded out with my adrenalin pumping and my hands ready for action. Big Ben, slower than me, but not by much over a short distance, was on my shoulder and ready to take someone apart.

The driver's window of his car was smashed in, and the windscreen had a big dent in it. Standing to the driver's side and ready to smash the next window, was a portly man with a bat and a ponytail.

'We want our money, Monica,' the man shouted as he lined up his shot. He wore ill-fitting dark blue jeans and a black leather jacket that was last in fashion in the late eighties. The ponytail did little for him, but a haircut wasn't going to be enough to improve his image.

'Boss,' said a man to his rear.

Just as I put a hand out to stop Big Ben - I wanted to speak with them first - Ponytail looked up and saw us. A smile lit his face. 'Well, well. What have we here? A couple of heavies. Monica hired you, did she? You might wish to reconsider your employment.' He lifted his free arm like a gameshow host showing the star prize. Behind him four more goons with bats were ready and willing to earn their keep.

'Just give me a moment,' I whispered over my shoulder. 'Then you can hurt them.'

'Don't take too long, Tempest. I don't want my rage to peak and begin to dwindle.'

'What?' asked Ponytail. 'What are you whispering about

over there? You should run away now unless you like having to suck all your food through a straw.'

'How much does Mrs Moore owe you?' I asked.

My question made Ponytail's eyebrows rise. Not for long though, he resumed the hardman pose and pointed the bat at me. 'I don't know you. My business is with Monica, and one never discusses business with the henchmen, that's just poor form.'

I'd hoped he might give me some answers, but as he lined up to take another shot at Big Ben's car, I said, 'Actually, your current business is with my friend. You've damaged his car, and I think he would like a word with you.'

My statement stayed his bat, but only so he could laugh, shifting his feet so he could face his lackeys, who joined in laughing because their boss was. None of them could feel the ground warming beneath their feet as the volcano got ready to erupt.

With a snort of amusement, I said, 'Go get 'em, buddy. I'll sweep up anything you miss.'

Big Ben pushed up his sleeves. 'Don't mind if I do.'

I let him get a few paces head start, then went after him. I had no concerns about letting him go at it alone; I'd seen him take on worse odds without breaking a sweat, but they were rude, and I wanted some exercise too.

They saw Big Ben coming and moved to intercept. They were big men. Even Ponytail, the boss, was over six feet and broad at the shoulder, but they were nothing compared to Big Ben. Their number advantage gave them confidence so when they should have all attacked at once, they let the nearest man step in and take his swing.

Big Ben caught it with one giant hand. It made a sound like a baseball hitting a glove at a hundred miles per hour and must have hurt, though Big Ben didn't flinch. He waited a heartbeat as surprise spread across their faces and he watched them. I knew what he was doing because I was doing the same thing: he was working out which would lead the attack, and which would hope his mates got the job done. It gave him an order in which to take them out.

They were spread out like a fan, three of them to Big Ben's left, Ponytail to his right, and goon number one still holding the bat Big Ben had caught. They suddenly looked less cocky, and they were all waiting for someone to move. However, they missed their chance to grab the initiative because Big Ben exploded into action first. With a sweep of his giant right foot, he kicked dust and dirt up at Ponytail, blinding him momentarily, but in the same movement, he yanked the bat toward him and folded his elbow up and high so it drove directly through the forehead of goon number one. It wouldn't do much visible damage, such as a strike to the nose would, but the man went down and didn't get up.

I darted left, dividing their attention, but two more were already swinging their bats at Big Ben's centre of mass. The clubbing blows ought to have broken his ribs on either side, but he jinked back once their swings were committed, waited the half second he needed for the bats to pass harmlessly through the point he'd just left and then ran at them. He shoulder charged the first, blasting him back ten feet by using sheer mass and inertia. It checked his own forward movement and allowed him to catch the second batsman with a flat hand to the top of his neck. The wild swing of his bat had carried the man all the way around so he faced the wrong way, and he never saw the blow coming.

Goon number four couldn't work out which of us to

watch. If he went for Big Ben, he had to turn his back on me. That, of course, was the whole point of me moving position. Fortunately for me, Ponytail had wiped the grit from his eyes and was coming at Big Ben's back. I think my friend was genuinely upset at not getting all five of them, but he gave me a nod of approval as he spun on the spot to place a hefty foot in Ponytail's midriff.

The boss doubled over with an outrushing of air just as I let the final man take his swing. I made sure I was light on my feet, bobbing and making it hard for him to find a target. Unable to pin me to take a good shot, what he should have done was abandon the bat, but he didn't have the confidence for that. When he finally screamed in rage and began his swing, the bat was way back behind his head. The effect was much like writing me an email in advance to tell me what he planned to do, and before the bat drew level with his head, I had closed the distance to him. I went for the bat, catching it low on the shaft and using my shoulder to smash it from his grip. It startled him, but not as much as my high elbow. My feet were splayed for balance, and I had my back to him. The bat was now in my right hand as my left arm whipped around and back. I intended to hit his throat. Unfortunately, he ducked or jerked in shock and my elbow, which I couldn't see because it was behind me, hit him square on the tip of his nose and turned it to hamburger.

Big Ben called to get my attention, 'Um, Tempest,'

'Yeah?' I was too distracted to look his way, checking around to see if any further threat existed. Whatever he wanted could wait two seconds.

Except it couldn't.

The wail of siren from a police car burst my bubble and

I let my shoulders slump in defeat as I looked again at the man I had just disarmed. Blood covered his face where his nose chose to explode. This was going to go badly.

Lost Time

Both cops bailed from their squad car with their batons out and their game faces on. Trying to see it from their point of view, what they could see was two men holding bats, a car which had clearly been attacked with a bat, and five men on the ground who appeared to have taken a beating from the two men still standing. The blood didn't help, but it wouldn't have made much difference at this stage if the worst they could show was a rather stingy smack to the bottom.

Big Ben and I knew the drill well enough. I'd lost count of the number of times the two of us, together or separately, had been arrested. I placed my bat on the ground, gently so it didn't make a lot of noise, and raised both hands so they could see them. In my right hand was my phone, hastily retrieved from my pocket because I needed to make a phone call.

Our breath, coming fast due to adrenalin and exertion, made billowing clouds of steam around our heads in the cold as we watched the cops come forward. They were determined, but nervous: we were offering no threat, but they couldn't know our intentions.

'Get down on your knees!' came the inevitable shout of instruction. 'Interlock your hands behind your heads.'

Neither of us moved. It was important to comply because it made the cops far more nervous to not do so. However, doing so was almost tantamount to an admission of guilt.

'We were defending our property,' replied Big Ben calmly. He meant his car, but they weren't to know that, and his ambiguity gave them a brief pause as they found their way around the imposing front gate and wall.

My call connected. 'Tempest. How's your day going?' asked Amanda conversationally.

'I'm about to get arrested with Big Ben. His car is undriveable. I have no time to discuss. I'll be in Swanley station I expect.' The cops were coming forward and my time was up. I murmured a goodbye, cut the call off without waiting to hear her response and put the phone away.

Big Ben's hands were out to his sides to show that he held no weapon and he was trying not to look threatening. Unfortunately, at six feet seven inches tall and wider than a refrigerator, he would need to put on a ballerina's outfit complete with pink tutu in order to achieve that. However, he would then fall into the dangerously deranged category.

'We were inside the house when we heard these five men attacking my car with their weapons. We disarmed them,' Big Ben explained.

From behind the houses to our left, two more wailing sirens filled the air as backup, which the first responders would have called the moment they saw us, sped to our location.

'I'm Tempest Michaels,' I tried hopefully. 'You might have heard of me.' I could see by their faces that neither officer had.

Stopping ten feet away with their batons raised in a pose they would have been taught in training, the lead officer repeated his command. 'Get down on your knees. This is your last warning, or we will use force.'

They had no reason to believe what we told them. The only safe course of action for the two officers was to disarm and neutralise everyone present and then sort it out. We could have disarmed them and returned their batons with a plea for calmness to ensue, but if that went wrong and one of the officers got hurt, it would go badly for us. And what about the backup racing towards us? We couldn't tackle them all.

With a sigh, I sank to my knees and placed my hands behind my head. 'I implore you to speak with the person inside the house. Mrs Monica Moore will explain the situation.'

Except she didn't.

The stone block driveway was damp and would ruin my trousers, but it was of little concern as two more squad cars screeched to a stop in the road outside the house. Since we didn't resist, it was over in seconds, cuffs clicking over our wrists as two cops quickly became six. I thought it likely one of the local residents made the call to the police when they saw Ponytail and his friends with their bats. I could find out later but waiting for Mrs Moore to appear was a fruitless endeavour because she was no longer at home.

When no one came to the door, the senior officer at the scene, a sergeant, asked, 'Are you the homeowners?' The question was addressed to Big Ben and me as we knelt a few feet apart.

'You're asking if we are a gay couple?' queried Big Ben. 'Seriously? You don't think I can do better than him if I was picking up men?'

He just couldn't help himself. 'We are not the homeowners,' I provided a sensible answer. 'We are, however, here at the homeowner's request.'

'There's no one home,' the sergeant pointed out.

I kept my tone patient and calm when I argued. 'And yet there was. Mrs Moore is my client. I do not know who these gentlemen are, but we heard them vandalising my colleague's car while we were inside speaking with Mrs Moore.'

Ponytail and his four friends were yet to say a word. An ambulance chose that moment to arrive, here to assess the extent of their injuries before the cops took anyone away.

My phone beeped in my pocket; an incoming text message I couldn't read with my hands cuffed. 'Would you mind?' I asked somewhat flippantly. It was the wrong thing to do.

Whether it was my attitude, the cold, or something else, the sergeant decided it was time to leave the area. Big Ben and I were loaded into the back of a squad car, that of the first two officers to arrive, and taken to the station.

In the front passenger seat, the officer looked us up. 'That's an impressive arrest record,' he said, looking at a hand-held tablet.

'How many times have I been charged?' I asked him. It was rhetorical question because I already knew the answer was never, but it made a point.

He snorted derisively, nevertheless. 'That hardly makes you innocent.'

The car was quiet for the rest of the journey, a short

one, thankfully, for there wasn't much room in the back with Big Ben stuffed in next to me.

So far as I was concerned, this was all lost time I could ill afford. The opposition, whoever they were, and I don't mean Ponytail, I mean whoever made the threats and invaded my parent's home, were operating freely and several steps ahead of me.

We were released without charge three hours later which was the time it took to process us, stick us in cells, get us back out of the cells to be interviewed individually, prove the car was Big Ben's, decide to release us, and go through all the rigmarole of giving us back our possessions.

Amanda was waiting in reception. Wise enough to understand the situation, she brought the case file with Mrs Moore's signature and payment to demonstrate we were engaged by her and had legitimate reason for being at the house.

The cops noted it, but Ponytail turned out to be a known local loan shark called Freddie Jackson. He was into all manner of illegal activity and known for using bats to make his point. His conversation with the cops would be more interesting than ours, I suspected.

'What happened to the client?' asked Amanda as we left the station. It was dark out already, the sun setting completely by four o' clock, and the streets were slick with a fresh shower which must have only recently passed.

'Beats me,' I quipped, feeling annoyed that Mrs Moore chose to abandon us. 'The loan shark was there to get money from her. I'd like to know how much because she appears to have lots of it.'

'Appearances can be very deceiving,' Amanda pointed out the obvious. 'You can see what she has spent, not what she has left.'

I nodded, acknowledging her point. 'Which could easily be a negative amount.' Taking my phone from my pocket, I checked the time: 1628hrs. I'd lost the whole afternoon, but that wasn't the dominant thought in my head. Nor were the six missed calls from my mother. My eyes were drawn to a text message from a number. That it was a number meant it wasn't a known contact, and yet I knew who it was from.

When my feet stopped moving of their own accord, Amanda and Big Ben kept going a pace before they noticed. I read the message again.

'We can see everything you do. We are better than you. You are going to lose. Leave the dead to be dead.'

I guess the concern I felt was visible on my face because both Amanda and Big Ben came back to see if I was okay. 'What is it, babe?' asked my girlfriend.

My teeth were clenched as I tapped out a reply and sent it. *'Who are you?'* Then I let them both see the screen, turning it so they were able to read it for themselves. Yet when my phone beeped, I snatched it away to read for myself. Too curious to resist, they shuffled around to look at it from either side of me.

'We are Undead Incorporated.'

It was a chilling answer, and that was most likely the point. They wanted to scare me off if they could. It was easier than killing me: convince me to stop and they could go about their business unchecked.

Not a chance.

'I missed lunch,' I announced loudly and with forced enthusiasm. 'Who fancies a curry?' If they were indeed watching me as the claim to see everything I did suggested, then they just saw me read their message and smile. Whether it was better to make them think I was scared, or that they scared me not one bit could be debated for hours. I felt more comfortable directly challenging them and that was what I planned to do. They believed they were better than me and perhaps they were. One thing I felt certain of: we were going to find out.

Phone Calls and Dinner

Big Ben's car was undriveable but all it needed was new glass and for the smashed glass inside to be cleaned away. Unfortunately, it was trapped inside Mrs Moore's grounds, and she was still not at home when we returned. Nor was she answering her phone and I didn't know what to make of that.

A little more than twenty-four hours ago she all but fainted in my office because the emotional drain of her undead husband returning overwhelmed her. She had money, or so it seemed, but there were loan sharks after her to pay back loans they believed she knew about. How much was she in debt to them for? Had she taken out the loans, or was it her husband? Did the debt have anything to do with his death? Questions were beginning to form a logjam in my head as more arrived and none of them got answered.

I tried Evan Allcorn yet again and began to feel like the fool who kept performing the same experiment while expecting different results. After dinner, I was going to change it up and go to his house.

Wait a second. How was I to get there? My car was being repaired – it got trashed by a gang of werewolves. Big Ben's car was also trashed, but even if it were ready to go, it was locked inside Mrs Moore's property. Big Ben had already scaled her wall against Amanda's advice – she felt getting arrested once in a day was sufficient – but there appeared to be no way to trigger the gate from the inside: it wasn't motion sensitive. Or, if it was, the motion sensor was switched off. Were it not for Amanda, we would be getting a taxi.

The curry house of choice was a place in nearby West Malling. That's nearby to where we live, not nearby to Swanley, I should clarify. It was an award-winning place with great food. We wouldn't be able to get a table if we arrived later, not even on a Tuesday evening, but our early arrival meant there was space for us.

'Beer?' asked Big Ben.

I wriggled my nose. I was laughably on edge; a beer would do me good. It would also soften my reflexes and that dictated my answer. 'I'd best not. I feel I must give credence to their threats. They might genuinely be watching our every move.'

He agreed and ordered sparkling mineral water for the table. Unable to relax, but finally finding I had the freedom to think, I checked my phone again and dealt with the first point of order: call my mother.

'Tempest!' she shrieked. 'Where have you been? I can't stay here another minute! I'm going somewhere where scantily clad women don't turn up at the door every few minutes. They all want to see Benjamin and I don't think they are here for cooking tips! It's ungodly!'

I could hear my father arguing pointlessly in the background. 'Mother, I implore you to stay where you are. I will be there soon. It is not safe for you to return home at this time.'

'That's what I said,' shouted my father so I could hear him.

'Well, it's not good enough, Tempest!' she snapped. Mother was easy to irritate. Everything that wasn't presented the way she wanted was irritating on the wrong day. The breakfast newscaster wearing a tie she didn't approve of was enough to get her started. No doubt the condom dispenser in Big Ben's kitchen was simply too much to take.

Okay, he doesn't really have a condom dispenser in his kitchen. It's in his en suite bathroom. I let her rant for another minute as she swore to walk home. I'd taken the precaution of hiding her car keys when she put them down this morning. I knew her too well to expect that she might behave. Dad would stop her from doing anything stupid if it came to it, but I didn't like that he was in that position because of my job. With a final promise that I would be there within thirty minutes, I ended the call.

'We should eat up so you two can get home,' said Amanda as the food arrived. Sizzling plates of spicy wonders plus rice, breads and sundries came to the table on an elegant trolley where two waiters expertly served them. I hadn't eaten Indian food for some time and the smells were making me salivate. Add to that the lunch I never got, and it might explain why I attacked my plate so ravenously.

While I stuffed my face, Amanda asked, 'Did you have an update from Jane yet?'

I slapped my forehead. So distracted by the text message threat from people who claim to be dead and a conversation with my mother complaining about naked women, I had completely forgotten to check my emails. Biting off a corner of naan bread and removing the flour from my fingers with a napkin, I touched the icon to access them.

My eyes zipped back and forth, absorbing what she wrote until I got to the piece of news I wanted to read.

Except it wasn't what I wanted to read at all.

Amanda and Big Ben waited for me to look up, both pausing their meals to see why my whole body had just sagged into my chair.

'They're both dead,' I told them. Amanda gave me a single raised eyebrow. 'The other two members of Dean Moore's team. The final name is,' I paused for effect and looked at Big Ben. 'Robert McTavish.'

'That's it,' he agreed, the name finally jogging his memory. 'I can see his face now.'

'Guess how both he and Vince Barnes died.'

Big Ben snorted a wry laugh. 'Fatal car crash?'

We fell silent for a moment, each of us working on the gravity of our situation. Someone had wiped out a whole special forces team, planning and staging their deaths so each looked like accidents and no one noticed anything amiss until Mrs Moore walked into my office yesterday.

'They were tailing her!' I blurted, sitting up in my chair again as if an electric pulse just operated my muscles. I still had the single raised eyebrow from Amanda but now it had a mimic on Big Ben's head. 'Mrs Moore comes to my office yesterday afternoon. She's with me for seventy-five minutes or so and when she leaves, I go for a sandwich. By then, they are tailing me.'

Big Ben frowned at me. 'You saw them?'

'No. Maybe. I thought I saw something, but when I looked, they were gone. Think about it though,' I begged at the unconvinced faces. 'How would they know to watch me? Unless they have triggers set up to alert them if someone looks at a particular website or performs a search for a particular person, they would have no reason to even know I exist. They weren't watching me; they just picked me up after Mrs Moore came to the office. There's a desperate dirty secret being hidden, and they are terrified that we will uncover it. They killed Dean Moore, and they were watching his wife.'

'Why would they be watching his wife?' asked Big Ben.

'That I don't know. It would help if she were available to answer some questions. I'm sure she'll phone soon,' I said, not convinced it would be true. 'She believed she was being tailed though. That was why she came in. Only, she thought it was her dead husband following her.'

Amanda nodded, but rather than agreeing with me, she asked, 'What else does Jane say?'

I picked the phone up again. I hadn't read all the way down and might not have done had Amanda not prompted me. It was a mercy she did, for otherwise I would have missed the scary stuff written at the end of her email.

Closet Monster

'We have to go right now,' said Big Ben. 'Waiting until the morning just gives them more opportunity to get ahead of us. Not only that, by doing so, we limit their targets. They can't get to your parents, not without a direct assault on a gated community less than a mile from Maidstone police station.'

'I can move in with Patience for a couple of days,' Amanda volunteered. 'That will make it hard for them to find me, and if neither Jane nor I go to the office, they won't be able to target us there either.'

Unsettled because I knew they were right. I looked down at my phone again. Jane's message read as follows:

Tempest, I found the final two members of the team you tasked me with finding, but I have to say this was one of the hardest searches I have ever performed. They just don't exist in the same way that a normal person does. The news, with which I'll start, is that the final name is Robert McTavish. Both he and Vince Barnes are deceased. Vince died on January 12th two years ago in a road traffic accident outside of Didcot. He was killed at the scene and buried in a closed casket. He was survived by his wife only; they had no children. Robert McTavish was killed in March of this year just outside Dundee. Likewise, he was survived by his wife and has no children.

That was where I originally stopped reading.

However, there is more. I can't find the wives. They have no listed home addresses. They did have. I can trace them to their husband's death and just beyond, but then both drop off the face of the Earth. Their media profiles no longer exist but they used to. By searching hard enough, one can find messages they sent to someone else, or posts they commented on which still exist on the profile of other people. Their own profiles have been erased and like I said, they don't live anywhere. It's like they were made to vanish within weeks of their husbands.

It was chilling stuff to read.

That's not all, and it gets worse. I went back and checked out the other members of the team again. When I first looked and found Edgar Salter, it didn't occur to me to look beyond him. Checking again, I find the same thing with his wife. He dies in a car accident. He's survived only by her and within weeks, there is no trace of her anywhere. Sharon Salter had a job as a hairdresser. I called the business and found a woman there who remembered her. According to her, Sharon just stopped coming to work and when she visited Sharon's house to see if everything was alright, someone else was living there. It's bizarre.

I don't know what this is Tempest, but it's unlike anything we have come across before. In an environment where people pretending to be ghosts and vampires is considered normal, this is weird.

74

Big Ben wanted to go. He felt that we needed to see things first hand by visiting the hometowns and finding people who used to know the missing members of Dean Moore's team. I couldn't argue. An entire special forces team had been wiped out and their wives made to vanish within weeks of their deaths. All bar one. Mrs Moore was still at large earlier today, and I doubted she had any idea about what happened to the previous wives, or even that the rest of the team were dead.

'Tempest,' Big Ben brought my attention back to the table. 'Mrs Moore vanished today. Quite inexplicably.'

'She might have run off when Ponytail and his friends showed up,' I argued.

He acknowledged my comment. 'But why then isn't she answering her phone? She might have left it behind. But how likely is it that she wouldn't find a way to contact you in the hours since?'

Amanda asked. 'Have you any missed calls from numbers you don't recognise?'

I already knew the answer, but I checked anyway. 'Her husband has been dead for two months. Jane suggested the others all went missing far faster than that.'

'Which could be just coincidence,' she countered. 'It might be time to go to the police, Tempest. If she has been snatched, we have a moral and legal responsibility to report it.'

I knew she was right; going to the police wasn't something that bothered me. I was only interested in solving the cases. About half of what we investigate leads to a criminal prosecution and the arrests are performed by the police. Every single time. What bothered me right now was just how little we knew. I couldn't remember feeling this much in the dark.

I tried to sum things up. 'Six men are disgraced and drummed out of their unit, but they are never sentenced. That means there was either not enough evidence against them to secure a conviction.'

'Or they just weren't guilty,' concluded Big Ben.

I shook my head. 'I think maybe they did do it – whatever it was. Or maybe one of them did it. Or all but one of them did it. They all carried the can because the last thing any of them would do – we're talking about brothers-in-arms here, remember – is spill the beans.'

'They would harbour a grudge though,' insisted Big Ben. 'Brother or not, if you were the one innocent member of the team and you were punished the same, that would eat away at you and the years might amplify the effect instead of diminish it.'

It was a theory that could fit this situation. 'It could be one of them, it could be half of them. We just don't know, but the theory that one of the six faked his own death and then went on to kill the others is plausible.'

'Or it could be the military cops who tried but failed to convict them for the heinous crime, whatever it was.' Big Ben was stretching, but he wasn't stretching all that far. 'Years later, and unable to accept that they got away with it and went on to live successful lives, the original investigators track them down and kill them.'

'What about the wives?' asked Amanda.

Big Ben shrugged. 'Could be they felt the need to tie off a loose end.'

I felt the possible truth in what he suggested. 'If we assume it is a member of the team who faked his own death, then it follows that he might need to kill the wives. The circle of wives might have remained in contact. Not all of them perhaps, but it was not uncommon for military wives to band together and form tight friendships that lasted. A member of the team kills a former colleague, lets the dust settle, then kidnaps the wife and murders her too, but takes his time to erase her life and take her money. Let's not forget the large insurance pay-out Mrs Moore cashed in. How many of the others had similar policies?'

Amanda started on her dinner again, getting it eaten so we could go. 'We need to answer that question,' she said. 'I think we need to get Jane back in front of a computer and commit to some hours of research. If they are targeting you, then they are targeting me and probably her as well.' A spoonful of king prawn biriyani went into her mouth the moment she stopped speaking.

My own appetite was stifled by my need to act. I wanted to go right now, but we still had Mr Best's closet monster to deal with. Maybe we would get away with that one, maybe no one would respond to his social media post.

But wouldn't you know it? My phone rang at that precise moment and the name displayed on the screen was Ramone Best Closet Monster since that that was how I chose to list him earlier.

'Mr Best, good evening,' I said as I snatched up the phone.

His wavering, wobbly voice replied, 'Yes, good evening. I dare say that we have caught a fish in the net you cast, Mr Michaels. Both my son and daughter called this evening to let me know they were popping in. They are bringing me a fish and chip supper of all things. Randomly, just like that, on a Tuesday. Are you still available to enact the plan you suggested?'

I almost blew out a breath of exasperation but held it in at the last moment. It was good to be busy - I would certainly moan if I had no cases to pursue - but I really didn't need this right now. 'How soon do you expect your children to arrive?' I asked.

'They said by six, but they are always late. How soon can you get here?' Mr Best enquired.

I glanced quickly at the clock and waved for the waiter as I made a sign for him to bring the bill. 'We can be with you before six,' I promised, thinking we would have to hustle to achieve it. 'Just in case your children arrive on time, please leave your back door unlocked. We'll slip inside and get in position.'

Less than five minutes later, stinking of glorious Indian spices, we were in the car and peeling away from the kerb. Amanda likes to drive fast, and she had the right car to do that in. However, the optimal handling for her nifty Mini Cooper did not include a calculation for a two-hundred-and-fifty-pound man to be stretched out across the back seat. Big Ben didn't fit in a Mini Cooper. He might have been okay if we threw the front passenger seat away. In so doing he could sit in the back and stretch his feet out into the front footwell. Instead, he was lying sideways across the whole rear seat.

Amanda complained, 'My car feels like I'm driving a barge. It's bad enough with Tempest in it. Now it feels like I'm smuggling gold bullion in the boot.'

'I was in the car earlier,' Big Ben pointed out. 'You didn't complain then.'

'I wasn't trying to get somewhere in a hurry then,' she growled as she downshifted and floored the accelerator. Her small car tried to leap into action but acted like a tiger with concrete boots: eager for action, but unable to comply.

The rain from earlier had chosen to return, a steady drizzle coated the roads and dripped from the trees as we wound our way through the countryside backroads to get to

Strood by the shortest route. There wasn't much traffic about, not on these roads. There would be plenty of people out and about in the more populated areas. This close to Christmas, eating out and meeting for drinks increased drastically and office parties abounded.

Our route deliberately avoided all the choke points where we might get stuck and delivered us to Mr Best's driveway a few minutes ahead of the six o'clock deadline.

'Any thoughts on where to leave the car?' Amanda asked. 'I can't take it onto his drive, or they will see it.'

'Big Ben and I can handle this. Call Jane and get to the office. We'll meet you there as soon as this is wrapped up. I don't think it will take long. I still think there might be someone watching the office so be vigilant, babe.'

She pulled to a stop fifty feet further down the road from his property, stopping in the street because there were no cars around. 'How will you get to the office? You want me to come back for you?'

I shook my head. 'It's only about three miles. We'll run if we have to.' I was getting out of the car but swung my head back to plant a kiss on her lips before I went. Big Ben clambered out from the backseat after me, leaning his own head across to Amanda for a kiss.

She placed a palm on his face and shoved it away. 'Get away from me, you big doofus.'

He got out chuckling. Headlights were coming up the road toward us. They were more than a hundred yards distant still, but since it could be Ramone's children, we skirted to the trees bordering the plush properties and slipped between them to sneak onto Mr Best's land.

Amanda's rear lights faded into the distance, and we were back on night ops; out in the dark, with the sound of the rain to cover our movements as we snuck up to the property. As discussed, Ramone's back door was unlocked.

Once inside, we stripped off our shoes to avoid leaving tell-tale wet footprints anywhere. Then we paused, listening for sound, just in case one of his children might have arrived by taxi or on foot, but the only noise was the sound of an open fire to accompany the heady smell drifting through the house.

Feeling ridiculous, I started to creep through the house like I was a child on my tiptoes. Behind me, Big Ben sniggered, and I turned to find him performing an exaggerated move as if he were a cartoon character from Scooby-Doo.

'You go first then, dickface,' I offered, stepping aside.

Before I could stop him, he called out, 'Mr Best, are you home?' It was the swift way to discover if the client's children were here, or to be discovered by them if they were.

He got lucky. 'Hello, boys. You did get here quickly,' Ramone said as he emerged from his living room. 'I think I just saw headlights pull onto the driveway. You had better get into position.'

We wasted no further words discussing what we planned to do, it was as simple as could be and all laid out earlier today. Mr Best announced to social media that he'd been having trouble with a monster in his closet and that it had been driving him nuts for weeks; scaring him at night and making him think he should take his children's advice and move out. Thankfully, a few nights ago, after trying several other rooms in the house, he'd moved into the smallest bedroom at the rear of the house and had enjoyed several nights uninterrupted sleep. He went on to joke about being old and yet still afraid of the monster in his closet.

The ruse appeared to have worked because his son and daughter were coming over to see him within hours of the post going out. Big Ben and I were going to hide in the closet ready to catch whichever of them excused themselves to visit the restroom only to sneak upstairs to fit a new popper device. It already had one, of course, Ramone's lie intended to make them think it had stopped working.

We hurried along the galleried upper landing lest our movement cause the floorboards to shift and squeak once they were in the house. In the back bedroom was a built-in closet, the kind that exists in the space between two rooms. It was a bit tight for two men, especially when one is the size of Big Ben, but we'd taken the time to check it out before we left the house this afternoon and knew what we were in for. Despite that, as I squeezed in next to my colleague, with only just enough room so we didn't have to hug each other, I hoped the wait wouldn't be a long one.

In the dark confined space, Big Ben rubbed his stomach. 'I think I might have some issues with the curry dinner.'

'What kind of issues?' I asked suspiciously.

'The kind that cause gas in copious quantities.'

'Don't you dare fart in here!'

'It wouldn't be my first choice,' he replied glumly. 'I'm just letting you know it's a possibility.'

'Duly warned. Nevertheless, if I hear an outrushing of gas, I'll be rushing out of here. Stuff the client and his closet monster. I'll catch them another way. I am not breathing in your butthole air.'

We both fell silent, listening for any sign of someone sneaking up the stairs. Ten minutes passed, then more. Faint murmuring noises of conversation drifted up to us, but no suggestion that our wait might be about to end. My bet was on the son. He would be the one to place the device and I worried silently if that was a sexist guess: he would do it because it required the use of a tool. It could just as easily be the daughter. For all I knew, she was an engineer.

Next to me, Big Ben was making grunting noises.

'Are you all right?' I asked.

'Yeah,' he hissed through clenched teeth. 'Just trying to hold up my end of the bargain.' His teeth weren't the only thing he was clenching.

A few more minutes went by, but as I began to grow impatient, for I had other tasks to which I needed to attend, a sound caught my attention.

'That was a stair tread shifting under someone's weight,' whispered Big Ben.

I didn't reply, silence was to be our companion now. Whoever it was approaching, they were doing so carefully and quietly, making the smallest amount of noise possible as they went about their despicable task.

Soon, they would open the closet and most likely scream in terror to find two large – okay one large, one extremely oversized – men hidden within. That would be game over for their little trick.

We waited, Big Ben groaned with the effort of keeping parts other than his vocal cords quiet, and we waited. Someone came into the room. The light stayed off, but they didn't open the closet door. I was holding my breath, not because I had chosen to do so, but because I was poised and filled with adrenalin.

A rustling sound reached our ears as we continued to wait and there were some odd mutterings as the person spoke to themselves. It was a man's voice, that much was clear.

Big Ben groaned again, intestinal distress and gaseous bloating beginning to sound like emergency venting might be required before something burst.

Finally, a shadow fell across the small gap between the closet doors as the client's son stepped up to open the doors. Eager to get it over, Big Ben raised his hands to leap out and scare the miscreant.

The doors opened, Big Ben opened his mouth to yell, 'Surprise!' or perhaps, 'Ha! There is a monster in this closet and it's in my trousers!' that would be a typical Big Ben opener.

However, outside the closet doors, and framed in the dim moonlight coming through the clouds outside, wasn't Mr Best's son.

It was a monster.

Big Ben squealed in fright like a little girl, jabbed out a giant right fist in reflex, and loosed about a quarter ton of methane inside the closet.

I ran for my life.

Not from the monster. Oh no. I was running from the stench of partially digested lamb bhuna.

The monster yelled out in pain as it went over backwards, swearing obscenities in English with a local accent to confirm what I felt sure to be true: Mr Best's son was inside the costume.

I flicked the light switch on, bathing the room in light from a single overhead bulb and poked my head out of the bedroom door when I heard running footsteps on the stairs. A man and a woman, both in their sixties, I guessed, were running up the stairs two at a time. They didn't see me, but they made me frown because their features were similar enough that I took them to be brother and sister. If the client's son was ascending the stairs, who was the closet monster?

The need for subterfuge well and truly behind me, I called out to my client. 'Ramone, are you there?'

His elderly voice echoed up the stairs as he ambled along. 'Coming, lad,'

'Who are you?' demanded the man I took to be my client's son.

I still suspected this pair to be behind the closet monster trickery, but we would know in the next few minutes. Taking a business card from my pocket, I held out my hand and gave them a courteous smile. 'I'm Tempest Michaels. I investigate paranormal phenomenon such as the strange occurrences your father has been suffering. He hired me to determine who was playing a trick on him.' I watched their faces as I spoke and knew for certain they were both guilty from their reactions. 'We have the perpetrator in custody,' I told them, making it sound all official. 'The police will be along soon.'

'What?' snapped the client's son angrily. 'Let me see.' He attempted to barge past me but met a hand that barred his progress. 'Get out of my way, man! Let me pass!' His face was turning crimson and spittle was forming at the corners of his mouth as his frustration grew.

'I think we should wait for the homeowner, sir,' I stated in a calm yet confident manner. 'Here he comes now.' Mr Best needed a lot more time to get to the top of the stairs than anyone else, but he got there all the same.

'We have your monster, Mr Best.' I glanced back inside the room where Big Ben stood over the costumed fool. The monster was on the floor still. He wanted to take his head-piece off, but Big Ben wouldn't let him. They'd been arguing ever since I came outside.

Closest to the door, the client's son sniffed the air. 'Why does it smell like lamb bhuna?' he asked.

Tempted to hold my breath but knowing I couldn't keep

it held for long enough, I went into the bedroom and stood to one side so the others could file in behind me.

No one followed. The son and daughter were trying to talk their way out of it. 'Father, this man is clearly a charlatan,' snapped his daughter, begging the old man to see sense.

'Yes, dad,' added her brother. 'You've been under a lot of stress lately. This daft monster thing has attracted a pair of con artists,' he stuttered. Then sensing a ray of hopeful genius in his lie, he grasped it. 'Yes! I bet that's it! A pair of con artists heard about … no, they saw your social media post and they rushed over here to convince you to let them catch the closet monster while they snuck this fellow in the costume in to play the part. Something went wrong and … and …'

'Can I please take this mask off now?' begged the monster. His head piece was a goldfish bowl with bug eyes inside. The bulk of the costume was a slimy-looking leather effect, intended, I suppose, to look like skin. The zip up the back of his legs kind of gave the game away, but it wouldn't have convinced a blind man in my opinion.

'No, I think you should keep it on,' argued the client's son. 'What's more, dad, I think you should let Sally and I escort both these men and whoever is in the costume from your premises right this very second.'

'But, dad,' complained the monster. 'I think he broke my nose.'

All eyes turned to the client's son, who, apparently, was also the monster's father.

When no one else argued, the monster reached up and yanked off the rubbery head to reveal a skinny ginger kid with spots beneath.

'Darren?' gasped Mr Best sadly.

'Hi, grandad,' the kid winced, touching his nose. There was blood all down the front of his face where Big Ben had exploded it. My colleague chose that moment to reach down and help the young man to his feet. The kid might have been nineteen, but he couldn't be much older than that.

'You did well,' said Big Ben. 'I've seen bigger men out cold from a blow like that. You should consider boxing.'

Darren didn't know what to make of that, but the game was up. My client's son had put his own son into a monster costume, and I didn't see how he could possibly hope to wriggle out of the truth now. I was about to wrap things up when Ramone raised his walking stick and used it to put a lump on his son's head.

His daughter flinched away, believing the crown of her skull might be next. 'What was the plan? Give me a heart attack?' Ramone raged at them. 'Are you that desperate for my money that you want me dead and out of the way? You'll not get a penny! None of you!' he spat.

'What about me, Grandad?' asked Darren as if he were somehow innocent.

Mr Best slowly turned himself around to fix the boy with a glare. 'What did your father tell you to do, eh? Jump out on me when I came to bed tonight? What did you think would happen? You're no fool, boy.' Ramone raised his walking stick again and I thought I might have to intervene – I couldn't let him whack a minor, but it was just a threat to get his grandson moving.

Mr Best's children ran for the stairs, fleeing the house with Darren waddle/running behind them in his stupid costume. My client leaned over the balustrade, damning his children for their greed and callousness, and threatening terrible things if they showed their faces again. The roar of a car moments later signalled their departure and it was clear the case was closed.

Mr Best sighed, but he didn't feel a need to discuss the subject further. 'Thank you, boys,' he acknowledged our efforts wearily. 'I'm just glad my Maureen isn't around to see how grasping they have become. Still,' he brightened, 'some good has come of it.'

'Oh?' I invited him to expand, assuming he would make a joke about needing to buy fewer Christmas cards this year.

'Well, I haven't written anything new in years. I just lost my inspiration I suppose, but you boys have given me an idea for a new series.' I tilted my head in question. 'I'm going to call it Blue Moon Investigations. It will be about a team of investigators who take on cases no one else would consider. In so doing, they solve nonsense paranormal mysteries but behind each case will be an idiot in a costume. I tell you what, it will be just like that cartoon I used to watch with my children. Oh, now what was it called? It had a big brown dog in it.'

'Scooby-Doo,' I supplied, helpfully.

He snapped his fingers gleefully. 'Yes! That's the one. They all went around in a big colourful van.'

'The Mystery Machine,' I helped again.

He fixed me with a serious look. 'You, ah, you don't have one of those, do you?'

I chuckled at the irony of his question and at the idea of driving around in a gaudily painted Volkswagon camper van. 'No. Currently, my friend and I are without a mode of transport. There have a been a couple of minor automobile related incidents.'

His eyebrows lifted. 'You need a car? You must take mine, my dear fellow.'

'I couldn't possibly,' I tried to argue.

'But I insist,' he insisted, with a stamp of his walking stick to emphasise the point. 'I'm much too old to consider ever driving it again. It hasn't moved in years. You'd be doing me a favour.' Wondering what pile of junk he might be trying to push on me, I tried once again to explain that it would not be appropriate, but he weathered my refusal without a bump. He was already leaving the room. 'I'll fetch the keys. We can call it payment for today if you like. You'll tell me it's too much, but you've inspired me and that can never be valued highly enough.'

Big Ben just shrugged his shoulders. 'We could do with some wheels,' he pointed out.

He wasn't wrong on that part. Reluctantly, and because he was already leaving the house by the back door, I followed Mr Best outside into the frigid air and across to his garage.

'I bought it on a whim when I was a younger man. My wife thought I must be having a midlife crisis, but it was all the fashion at the time. I must say, I loved driving it. I shall be pleased to know it is going to a good home.'

My curiosity was piqued and for good reason. Nevertheless, I expected to see an Austin Allegro or a Hillman Imp inside. I wasn't expecting the pristine series 1 Lotus Esprit. My eyes popped out on stalks as I scanned around his garage to find a different car, the one he intended to give away because this couldn't be it.

'It doesn't have a lot of what you might think of as modern features,' he said in an apologetic tone. The windows wind down, there's no satellite navigation ...'

I wanted to rip the keys from his hand and drive away before he could change his mind, but I knew I could never accept such a generous gift. The fibreglass body on the Lotus Esprit ensured the cars never rusted but also meant they were prone to cracking from even the slightest knock. Not so this one. It looked as if it had just left the factory.

'Do you have any thoughts about what I should call the first book?' Ramone asked, and, as if sensing I was about to walk away, he reached out to grab my right wrist and dumped the car keys in it. 'Take good care of it, Mr Michaels and it shall be your noble steed.' When I opened my mouth to speak, he held up a warning finger. 'I only want to hear your suggestion for the title of the first book, sir.'

I let my shoulders slump and accepted the car in lieu of payment. Maybe he was right, maybe our paths crossing had given him something he couldn't buy. The name for a book? A grin curled the side of my mouth. 'Perhaps you should call it Paranormal Nonsense.'

'Paranormal Nonsense,' he repeated three times, trying it on for size. 'You know, I rather like that. You should let the oil pressure come up before you start to drive her. Just push the garage doors shut behind you. I'll lock up later. If you don't mind, I think I ought to get back inside by the fire.' On his way out of the garage side door he paused to say. 'Thanks again, boys. It's been a strange old day, but if you'll excuse me, I'm off to write a masterpiece.'

Left alone in the garage, I stared down at the car keys in my right hand until Big Ben thumped me on the shoulder. 'We should get going. You told your mum you would be back shortly and that was more than two hours ago.'

He was right, and for once I hadn't forgotten. But his reminder gave me an idea.

Undead

From the car, Big Ben called Amanda's phone. She was at the office as expected but we weren't heading there anymore. We were going to Big Ben's place where we could hunker down together and work our way through the problem. My parents and my dogs were there, and it was less exposed than the office.

Jane had just arrived but both ladies would pack up and head to Maidstone now.

'Hold on,' said Amanda. 'How will you get there?'

'It's a secret,' whispered Big Ben enigmatically, then disconnected. Turning to me as he ran his hand along the car's interior, he said, 'I don't know how you do it.'

'Do what?'

'Fall into a bucket of turds and come out smelling of roses all the time. I mean, how is it you are driving this amazing classic car? How is it that you are dating such a fine woman?' It was perhaps the first time I had ever heard him sound jealous.

'Amanda is fine,' I agreed for something to say.

He stared out the windscreen wistfully. 'Sometimes you make me wonder if I haven't got it all wrong.'

Startled by his revelation and hoping he wasn't about to say he'd decided to settle down, I kept my mouth shut. Honestly, I worried the planet would simply stop spinning if he changed his ways. Mercifully, I spotted familiar taillights ahead as we swept along the A228 toward the motorway.

'There's Jane.' I pointed out.

'Yeah, I think that's Amanda ahead of her.' Mini Coopers are two a penny, but it probably was her, the ladies driving in convoy when they left the office.

On the motorway, I pulled around them both, the old, but well-maintained British sports car easing through the gears and surging ahead when I pressed the accelerator. It made me wonder what it might feel like without a passenger in it. Slowing, as I pulled level with Amanda, Big Ben shot her a wave, so I got to see her wide questioning eyes just before I hit the pedal again to surge ahead. I was breaking the speed limit to do it; something I rarely do unless the situation demands it, which this didn't, and I slowed again as we cruised toward the off ramp.

'Where did you get this car?' Amanda wanted to know when we were all safely inside Big Ben's gated community.

'The client gave me it as payment,' I admitted.

A sly grin crossed her face. 'It belongs to the firm then?' She was angling to get her hands on it.

'Ha! I don't love you that much,' I laughed, but my joke silenced her; declaration of the 'L' word stunning her and making Big Ben and Jane decide they had a sudden need to go inside.

The moment they were out of earshot, she said, 'You don't love me enough to let me have the car, but you do love me.' She wasn't asking me; she was making a statement.

Now I was standing on loose ground. 'It was just a thing to say,' I tried, but the words sounded weak, and she didn't believe them.

She came closer, getting into my personal space. 'I figured I would be the one to say it first. Girls are supposed to be the soppy ones.'

'That's just outmoded stereotyping,' I murmured. 'I … It's not soppy anyway. Men are capable of feeling love. I think you'll find men write more love songs than women.' I was trying to make light of the situation, moving the conversation on so we could go inside and not talk about it. If I had a handy shovel, I might have started digging a grave to bury myself in just so she would stop looking up at my face.

'I love you too, Tempest.'

My heart thudded in my chest and Mr Wriggly rubbed a pair of imaginary hands together with glee. We kissed in the moonlight outside Big Ben's building and though a chill wind blew, neither one of us felt it. Until the kiss ended.

'I need to get inside,' she gasped. 'It's got to be five below freezing out here.' Next to the water, the cold was amplified, and I agreed with her desire to get into the warm.

We arrived upstairs to an argument. Unsurprisingly, the voice doing all the arguing was my mother's. The dogs were outside, looking up at the humans and most likely wondering what was going on. They spotted me and zipped over the tile to greet me, their little tails wagging madly. I picked them both up so I had something to do while I listened to my mother's ranting.

'I've worn through the soles of a pair of slippers just answering the door today,' she growled at Big Ben. He had his hands cupped to his front and in them were what looked like raffle tickets.

'Was there a Chantelle among them?' Big Ben asked hopefully, his melancholy from earlier showing no sign of itself now. 'Tall, willowy, long blond hair like a shampoo advert model?' He looked to see if that rang any bells.

'I had to ban Tempest's father from answering the door because all the little hussies were making him dribble. One of them turned up naked!'

'She wasn't naked,' my father argued.

We were outside of Big Ben's door where my mother had undoubtedly ambushed him. Jane had slipped around them and gone inside, but Big Ben's route into his own property was blocked by the imposing form of my mother.

'She was naked!' mum snapped.

'Which one?' asked Big Ben. 'Did you get a name?'

'That's what the raffle tickets are for!' shrieked my mother. 'I found a pack in the bottom of my knitting bag from the last church social. They use them to raise money for charity,' she growled as if any other use was dirty. 'I made each of the … women,' she decided to call them, probably after rejecting several other terms which she thought more appropriate but couldn't lower herself to utter, 'write her name on one half of the raffle ticket and take the other half home. Now you have all their names and can call them yourself. When I agreed to hide here,' she spat the words in my direction, 'I did not expect to become a madame for a harem!'

I'd had enough. 'This isn't your house, mother,' I pointed out, forcing her backward so we could get inside.

'I keep telling her that,' sighed dad.

'You don't get to make the rules,' I reminded her, a touch of irritation colouring my words.

'And that,' he sighed again.

'You won't have to put up with it for long.'

Dad snorted a wry laugh. 'It sounds like you are reading my script.'

Mum wasn't done complaining. 'It had better not be long. The whole house smells like a prostitute's handbag, and I found condom wrappers in the trash.'

'What were you doing going through the trash?' I asked her accusingly. The house smelled like it had electronically controlled air fresheners in it – because it did. Big Ben went to the refrigerator and took out a bottle of chilled white wine. Mum took a large glass when he silently offered it and we heard little from her after that.

The moment she retired to the living room to watch a gameshow, dad and I both breathed a sigh of relief. 'How bad was it today?' I asked him.

He laid his head flat on the kitchen counter. 'You remember the time she opened the refrigerator and found a snake had come home in her groceries from the market?'

'Yeah, Rachel and I got into trouble for suggesting it evolved in the gloop at the bottom of the salad crisper.'

He laughed at the memory. 'Yeah. She went on about that for weeks and wouldn't open the fridge in case there was another. Well, today was like that.'

I patted him on the shoulder in sympathy.

We were all dotted around Big Ben's breakfast bar, a marble countertop with a sink and food prep area on one side and four seats on the other. There were five of us, but my father felt he'd spent enough of his day sitting on his backside already. He was going to stand for a while. To that end, he made drinks while the rest of us settled in to trawl the internet and dark web.

On a chalkboard Big Ben usually used for recording

what groceries he needed, we set out what we didn't know. It was a long list.

'It's the vanishing of the wives that I want to look at,' said Jane. 'I want to see if I can find communication between any of them. It might be a dead end. If they didn't use social media and communicated using their phones, I'll never find it. It's got to be worth a shot though.'

'What specifically are you looking for?' I asked.

She looked up from her screen again. 'Anything where they indicate they stayed in contact and then anything about the deaths and the disappearances. Were they scared? Did any one of them have a sense that someone was coming for them? Were they offering conjecture about it?'

It was a good place to start.

Big Ben asked, 'Can I use your laptop?' I passed it to him without questioning it. He had a tower system set up in a different room, but it was more convenient for us to all stay in one place where we could bounce ideas off each other. 'I'm looking at flights to Scotland,' he explained. 'Rob McTavish was the most recent death not including Dean Moore. It might still be fresh in people's minds. We could talk to people he worked with, maybe turn up some family members who know something about the crash. He might have talked to someone if he was concerned about the other members of this team being killed. I might even find his local pub and be able to show some pictures around. Do we have any recent pics of them? I'm thinking, if there was a conspiracy between some of the team members, they might have met. Or, if it was just one of them, and they did fake their death, we might be able to eliminate them one at a time. Might as well start with the furthest point, right?'

Amanda dealt with the call to the police in Swanley to report Mrs Moore as missing. It was a paperwork exercise only as we had not one shred of evidence to be able to claim anything had happened to her. But while she did that and refused the invitation to file the report in person at the station, I wasted a few minutes trying to call Mrs Moore and Evan Allcorn with the exact same result I got every previous time I'd tried. It wasn't so late that I couldn't go to Evan's address to see if he were there. But I could only do one thing at a time and what we were doing seemed more pertinent right now.

Half an hour later, mum wandered out looking for more wine. The bottle she took a glass from, she'd then emptied. She wanted a snack too. Big Ben invited her to help herself, and asked me, 'Do I book this?'

His laptop screen was turned my way. He had flights into Dundee airport in the morning. It meant an early start, but we could get up there and be back the same day. It might prove fruitless, but we had to try something. We were on the back foot and struggling.

My dad had a question, 'How soon before the police will consider Mrs Moore as a missing person?'

Amanda didn't look up when she replied, 'Two days, but we have to follow up to confirm she is still missing. Then they will begin the process of questioning what might have happened to her. Otherwise, without us prompting, they would call us after seventy-two hours to ask for an update.'

'If the Undead have her?' I started.

Jane raised an eyebrow. 'The Undead?'

'We have to call them something. They called themselves Undead Incorporated. They claim they are dead and want to be left that way, yet they can use a phone to convey the message.'

'Okay.' Big Ben picked up the chalk to write it on the board. 'The Undead it is.'

I picked up where I left off. 'Anyway, if the Undead have her, I doubt she has three days. They'll be making her disappear ...' I tailed off as an idea hit me. 'Jane, can you find her social media and online presence, please. I want you to benchmark it and keep an eye out for anything disappearing.'

'Sure thing. I can set automatic notifications for that.' I'm sure she could. I couldn't, but such things were a doddle for her.

'Booked,' announced Big Ben. You and I have a flight out of Stansted at 0515hrs tomorrow morning. We need to be ready to board at 0445hrs.'

Dad whistled. 'That's an early start.'

He wasn't wrong and I thought about how little sleep I'd got the night before. It wasn't yet nine o'clock, but dad was yawning like he needed to go to bed, and I felt quite similar. When I yawned, it set Amanda off, which then triggered Big Ben.

I pushed on for another hour, trying to find information about Mrs Moore and her husband's business, about Evan Allcorn and what might have happened to him, and about Dean Moore's team in general. There wasn't much to find until I turned up a hit on LinkedIn. Why I hadn't thought to look there before I couldn't tell you, but there was Evan Allcorn, the former director of Control Systems Engineers. His current employment status was listed as field service engineer which I knew to be a catchall title for jobs both grand and trivial. His role looked trivial, and when I looked at National Controls, the firm for which he now worked, he wasn't a member of the Board, and they appeared to have a turnover barely more than a decent wage for one man. He'd fallen a long way. Just what had happened to the firm after Dean died, and did it have anything to do with Ponytail and the money he wanted from Mrs Moore?

Amanda touched my arm. 'You should get to bed. Lord knows I need to.' Mum and dad had already gone. Big Ben had closed his laptop ten minutes previously which left only Jane staring at her screen.

Sensing I was going to ask, she said, 'Don't worry about me. I am full of caffeine. I couldn't sleep if I tried. This whole thing is starting to irk me anyway, so I'm just going to keep on going until I find a thread to pull at.'

I thanked her for her diligence and took Amanda to bed where neither one of us had the energy for anything but sleep.

Okay, Mr Wriggly had the energy, but Amanda knew I needed to get up in less than five hours so it was a hard no to his very hard *yes, please.*

Haggis for Breakfast

WEDNESDAY, DECEMBER 21ST 0630HRS

It was cold in Scotland. Much colder than the southeast corner of England some five hundred miles due south from Dundee. However, neither of us made comment as we searched the parking lot for our hire car. It was under a foot of snow where the climate, especially on the east coast, was much the same as one would find in Scandinavia. Few realise that Scotland is more northerly than Denmark and only stays as warm as it does because of currents flowing upward past its western coastline.

Using our coat sleeves, the snow found its way to the ground, and we darted inside the car where the wind and cold could be shut outside. To give Big Ben some leg space, I'd thrown some money at the task and hired a Mercedes G Wagon. This also gave us some sensible off-road capability since we were heading into the Scottish countryside where the snow might not be cleared at all.

Rob McTavish was recorded as living in Dundee but in actuality, he lived just outside the large Scottish city in the village of Barry. Barry lay on the east coast where Scotland met the North Sea. Once we were clear of the city, there was nothing to see for miles but trees and rolling hills.

At 0330hrs, when we were leaving the house, Jane was still up, and I paused to talk to her while Big Ben made sandwiches in the kitchen. Seeing Jane at that time of the day was a slightly surreal experience because her wig was off. So too her makeup, and the wipes used for the task were sitting still on a crumb-laden plate just beyond her laptop. I know in my head that there is a man hidden beneath the petite blonde woman's clothing, but James is so rarely seen these days that I sometimes forget. The short dark brown hair where a mop of blonde can usually be found, and a trace of overnight stubble made my bleary eyes do a double take.

'You still going?' I had asked rhetorically.

I got a slow nod in response and thought that was all he/she – I couldn't decide what I ought to call him/her since I was now looking at a man in a dress, with fake boobs and ladies jewellery – was going to say on the matter. Leaving him/her to it, I was surprised when he/she then said, 'I might be onto something.'

I asked what it was, but he/she said there was nothing worth sharing yet because it might prove misleading. I would get an email in due course if there was anything to report. In the meantime, Jane/James, sent me a picture of Rob McTavish. It was the one from his obituary which his wife or a member of the family must have picked out. It wasn't the best picture we could hope for since he wore uniform in it and had to be at least ten years out of date. It was all we had for now.

Driving to Barry, and going slow in deference to the conditions, though the main road we chose to follow had been cleared of snow and gritted, it still took only forty minutes. We arrived at a time we considered too early for knocking on doors.

As luck would have it, coming through the centre of the village, we passed a greasy spoon style diner which opened for breakfast at 0700hrs each day. To our surprise, there was only one table available inside; the windows were fogged with condensation to stop us seeing inside, yet we expected it to be mostly empty at this time on a Wednesday morning.

'This place is popular,' Big Ben commented to the man at the counter. The last table was next to the serving hatch where heaping plates of breakfast appeared moments later. They weren't ours, Big Ben had yet to order, but the pile of sausage, egg, beans, and more appealed to my sleep deprived brain.

He knew better than to ask for a full English – not the done thing in Scotland – but got two haggis platters which came with an abundance of everything a growing boy could want. Taking his seat, Big Ben said, 'Most of the chaps in here are from a new container port they are building just up the coast. They are on long contracts according to the chap behind the counter. His breakfast business is booming it would seem.'

'Did you show him the picture?' I asked. It was what we were here for.

A pot of tea arrived courtesy of the man behind the counter, and I expected Big Ben to delay his answer until the man had gone again. He chose to pull him into the conversation instead.

'You said you recognised Bob McTavish, didn't you?' he reminded the man. 'This is my colleague, Tempest. We were both with Bob in Iraq.'

'Aye, I knew him. Everyone around here did. He was the only person in the village in the army at the time, and his sister made sure everyone knew about his exploits. You boys were SOS too then?' He looked at Big Ben, who was at eye height with the man now that he was sitting. 'You sure look like you were.'

We chose to do what any of the blades would have done and neither confirmed nor denied what we might have been. I was too busy focussing on the fact that Rob McTavish had a sister. 'Is his sister still living here?' I asked.

Big Ben said, 'I was just getting to that part,' then fell silent so the man could answer.

'Aye, she lives on Monteith Road just across the way. Just be careful when you speak to her, ye ken? She's a little off some days.'

'In what way?' I sought to clarify.

The man pulled a face as if wishing he hadn't mentioned it and now looking for a polite way to explain why the lady was a bit bonkers. 'She doesnae believe her brother is dead,' he explained. 'She's got this crazy conspiracy theory going about a government cover up because he was recruited to be a secret agent or something. She says his death was faked so he could become a ghost operative for them.'

The revelation hit me like a lightning bolt coming through the ceiling. Big Ben had been right to suggest we come here. We'd spoken to one person and already had more information than we could have gathered at home.

'What about his wife?' Big Ben asked when I failed to raise a question myself. 'Does she still live around here?' It was a leading question to get the man talking since we already knew she vanished right after his death.

'His wife?' the man repeated. 'I don't rightly know. I don't poke into other people's business, ye ken? I haven't seen her in a while, but she wasn't from around here. Maybe she went home.' A call to get his attention came from a table on the other side of his small diner; someone wanted more coffee. He gave us a nod to excuse himself. 'Your breakfasts will be right out.'

When he moved away, Big Ben and I locked eyes. 'His sister thinks he is still alive,' he repeated the big news.

'How come Jane didn't find his sister?' I asked the air. Jane finds everything. With the exception of financial records, which can be very tricky to access, Jane is a whizz at delving into a person's background. I decided to call her while we waited for our food. Turning down the volume on my phone and putting it on speaker so we could both hear her, I placed it flat on the tabletop.

Big Ben poured the tea. 'Do you think she will be awake?'

He made a good point. It was breakfast time, so everyone else in his suite would be up, but she was yet to go to bed when we left. Too late to stop it from ringing at her end, it was answered before I could consider terminating the call.

'How's Scotland,' asked Jane around a yawn. 'Did you find his sister yet?'

'Err, Hi, Jane,' I replied. 'That's why I'm calling. I need some information on her. Obviously, you found her.'

She yawned again; we could hear her fighting to make it stop so she could speak. 'That's what I was working on when you left. I found his obituary – that was easy – but finding anything else was proving difficult until I stumbled across a report in a local paper. Local to Dundee, that is, where Robert McTavish lived and died. Six weeks after his death, his sister bumped into him in the street of a local town. It made the paper because she had a heart attack and nearly died. Witnesses said a man ran away as she collapsed to the ground. No positive identification was made, but she remained adamant it was him and the police started a brief manhunt – it seems he left this mortal coil with a court case for assault hanging over his head.'

'Anything on his wife?' I asked.

'Greta McTavish left the area immediately after his funeral. I think she went to live with her parents in Aberdeen and you're about to ask me why.' She yawned again and the man serving food came back past us to snag two steaming plates from the kitchen serving hatch.

'Hold on a second,' I begged Jane, while he served our breakfasts. 'We're just getting breakfast,' I explained.

'Food,' she commented wearily. 'That sounds good.'

With the plates delivered and a query about a fresh pot of tea answered, he bustled back to the counter where new customers were ready to order. 'You were telling us his wife left the area,' I prompted.

Jane yawned again, and I hoped she would go for some sleep when we finished the call. 'She registered at a library in Aberdeen, or at least, someone using her name did and it was less than a mile from the address for her parents.'

I said, 'I'll take that as proof.'

'It feels solid,' she agreed. 'She left the area, but she didn't look for a new job, she didn't tell any of her friends she had moved, not from the traces I could find on social media she didn't anyway, and she wasn't there very long. He died in May, she appeared in Aberdeen in June, and there's no sign of her after July.'

'What date was the newspaper article about his sister seeing him?' asked Big Ben, a forkful of egg and bacon halfway to his mouth.

'The first of August.'

I believed it. That was a poor conclusion for a detective

to reach; I ought to be questioning everything until I could be sure of anything. Otherwise, I could be drawn down random rabbit holes and chase shadows while achieving nothing, but since the start of this – which was less than two days ago – my assumption had been leaning towards one of the team being responsible. It could be any of them, but it was beginning to look like it could be Rob McTavish. Did he have my client? Was she being tortured for passwords to her bank accounts while I ate haggis and fried egg?

If she were, then I was five hundred miles from wherever he had her stashed.

'Anything else?' I asked, shoving my senseless worries to one side.

'Only that her mortgage went unpaid, and her bills stacked up. The house they lived in is still empty, repossessed by the bank, but that process took until last week so you might find there are clues still in it,' she told us hesitantly because she was suggesting we break and enter. 'Now, I really need to get a couple of hours shut eye. Do you really think I should stay here instead of going home?'

I nodded my head though she couldn't see the action. 'Yes, Jane. It might be Rob McTavish behind this, it might be someone else, we just don't know, but they were all experts with explosives, and deadly killers. We've had friendly warnings so far. The best way to defuse them, is to take away their targets. Get some rest, we'll be back later today and maybe we'll know more by then.'

She was too tired to present an argument and probably believed I was right anyhow. We disconnected and I fell upon my breakfast. Haggis isn't impossible to find in England, it just feels like an odd thing to purchase, especially for a man living alone. Asking myself when I last ate it, I couldn't supply an answer, but it had to be more than five years. What I had on my plate had a short life-expectancy, the last few crumbs getting mopped up minutes later with a piece of toast.

Big Ben's plate was just as empty as mine and it was time to go.

Dead Man's Sister

Diligently efficient as always, before she got into bed, Jane sent an email with addresses for Rob and his wife's repossessed house, and for his sister, and for the cemetery in which his body was to be found.

We took a drive by his house. A foot of snow covered the front lawn of the small, terraced cottage. The row of houses appeared to be hewn from stone as if the land had vomited the rocks and man simply put in some windows. I knew there was a name for the style, yet it escaped me when I tried to recall it.

The snow probably covered an overgrown lawn, left to go wild when Greta walked out. Why did she go to her parents? Did they file a missing person report when she disappeared? Leaving Big Ben to drive, I sent a few of my questions to Amanda, begging her to find the answers, and tackled some of them myself. Greta's parents might be able to provide pivotal answers or might know nothing at all. I wouldn't be able to find out until I had their phone number and address. We were only sixty miles from Aberdeen so if it came to it, we could go there and ask them in person.

First, we were going to quiz Rob's sister.

Living in the same small town, it didn't take long to get to her address, the Satnav system delivering us to her door where we could see lights on inside. I didn't have a picture for her but felt confident I was addressing Alice Cumber when she opened the door. From the email Jane sent, I knew her to be forty-three years old. Beyond that I knew nothing. The woman who answered the door was about that age, roughly five and half feet tall and wide at the hips. Her perfectly straight dark auburn hair had been yanked into a tight ponytail though wisps escaped to give her a halo where the bare lightbulb behind her head shone through it.

There was a step up to her house which placed her at my head height.

'Good morning,' I gave her a smile. 'My name is Tempest Michaels. This is Benjamin Winters,' I indicated Big Ben with my right hand. 'We are old army buddies of your brother. We knew him from his days in the SOS.'

Her curious expression changed instantly at the mention of her brother and his former career as she went from wondering what we might be trying to sell in the predawn gloom, to excited that she might be able to retell her tale. 'Oh, goodness, come in, come in.' She beckoned us to follow her and backed away from the door. As we crossed her threshold, she asked, 'Do you work with him now? Have you brought me a message from him?'

I hadn't expected this, but so convinced was she that her brother was alive and working for a secret government branch, she invited us in because she assumed we were the same.

Once the door closed the cold outside once more, I said. 'I'm afraid not, Mrs Cumber,'

'Oh, call me Alice, dear. You said your name is Tempest?' I nodded. 'That's a new one on me. I've never met a Tempest before.' She was talking as she led us into her house. The front door opened into a narrow hallway that ran past the stairs to link with other rooms. She started shouting orders before we reached the end of the hall. 'Bianca! Get to school! Teddy, you too!'

As we came into the kitchen, two sullen-faced teenagers, carbon copies of their mother, were sloping toward the back door. Neither kissed their mother goodbye, nor spoke a word as they traipsed outside and into the snow.

Alice growled a few expletives at their back through the closed door and began clearing up their abandoned, dirty breakfast things. 'It's the last day of school. You'd think they'd be excited to go for once,' she complained.

I expected she would continue complaining about the trials of motherhood, and was ready to divert the conversation, but she dumped the dishes into the sink and said, 'What did you come here for, boys, if it's not to deliver a message? Did he get killed for real this time? Where did they send him?'

Unsure how best to broach the subject, and get from her that which I wanted, I tried the direct approach. 'Mrs Cumber, I believe your brother, Rob McTavish, is still alive and that his death was faked.'

She threw her arms in the air. 'Hallelujah! Finally, someone who believes me.'

'You saw him a few weeks after his funeral, didn't you?'

'Yes, I did,' she snapped irritably. 'No one believes me. They have been treating me like some kind of local lunatic.

I lost my job at the pub; jobs aren't easy to come by around here, you know?'

'I'm sure,' I acknowledged with a tinge of sympathy in my voice. 'Can you retell the tale for us?' I begged. 'Give us all the detail.'

I got a quizzical look for a moment, but she flipped her eyebrows, extracted a cigarette which she lit on the gas hob, then with a puff of pungent smoke, she leaned against the cooker and took us back to August 1st. 'I saw him across the street when I got out of my car, I was in Carnoustie, just along the coast road. They have a second-hand shop there that specialises in school uniform. Anyway, I saw him across the street. He had a hoody on, and the hood pulled right up to cover his face. I knew it was him though. He's my little brother. I called his name, and he twitched, but kept going. So I ran after him. My heart started beating out of my chest, and when I grabbed his arm and spun him around, that's when it stopped. He'd been dead for more than a month. I cried my eyes out at the funeral, unlike that bitch wife of his, but he wasnae dead at all. He was right there on that street in Carnoustie.'

She took a long draw on her cigarette, sucking down the foul smoke as her hand shook with emotion. We remained quiet, waiting for her to continue though fresh questions were already poised on my lips.

She patted her chest. 'The doctors said I shouldnae smoke, especially after the heart attack. Stupid heart. If it hadn't given out, I would have been able to ask him what was going on. He spoke to me though. He called out for help as I collapsed, and he spoke to me. He said, "Alice I'll come back for you when I can. I have a job to do." That was all. I think I lost consciousness at that point, but his words stayed with me. That's what I thought you were here for today, to collect me or to tell me more about what he is up to.'

I wanted to ask how certain she was, but I already knew her answer would be absolutely convinced to the point no evidence to the contrary would sway her. Instead, I asked, 'Who identified his body?'

She puffed out a lungful of smoke. 'That would be his wife. I only found out later the same day. He was killed in the morning. His fault they said. He pulled out in front of a van, and he died there at the scene.'

Cringing inside that I had to pose the next question, I kept a straight face when I asked, 'Do you know if there were injuries to his face?'

Alice Cumber paused with smoke coiling slowly from her mouth and her eyes locked on mine. 'How do you know that?'

'I don't know,' I admitted. 'It's a logical conclusion. Your brother's body is identified by his wife, but you know that he is still alive, so whose body went in his coffin and who was it that your sister-in-law identified? I guessed that there had to have been facial injuries, otherwise how could she get it wrong?'

How indeed? Echoed in my head.

'I cannae say who is in the coffin. I wanted his body exhumed but no one would listen to me. I lost my job when I tried to dig his body up myself. It caused a bit of a scandal, and the publican didn't like folks talking when they should be drinking.'

'Have you had any contact with your sister-in-law since she left the town?' asked Big Ben.

'That cow? No. I'll not call her, and she'd never call me. I was beneath her always. She had ideas way above her station. Always acting like her ship was about to come in.'

'Do you know why she left?' I pushed her to give us more information. 'And why would she leave so suddenly?'

Alice shook her head. 'I've nae idea. One day she was there, the next she wasnae.'

The whole thing was perplexing. I was going to have to go to Aberdeen, that much I was certain of now. There was time to kill before our flight later this afternoon, and that was how we would use it. Talking to Alice was useful but only to confirm what I already believed. I had more questions though, and one of them was a biggy.

'Alice, when your brother came back from Iraq in 2003, there was a scandal hanging over his head and an investigation into war crimes was threatened. Did he ever talk to you about what happened?'

Big Ben added, 'Did he ever talk about his team? Did he speak with them do you know?'

'Oh, aye,' she replied. 'They remained proper friendly. He never really talked about Iraq, or about anything he did in the Army, and it was years after when I found out he'd been kicked out of the SOS. I don't know if it bothered him. I guess it must have but he was always talking about the future not the past. They came to visit him a few times over the years – the boys from his team.'

Switching tack, I came from another angle, 'You said his wife didn't cry at his funeral.' It wasn't a question, just a reminder of her statement because I felt sure she would want to expand.

'That's right. She didnae. Cold hearted, callous bitch. She was most likely trying to hide her grin and the life insurance pay-out she was about to receive.'

A lightbulb flickered into life above my head. 'Life insurance?' I repeated casually. 'Your brother had taken out a worthwhile policy?'

'Oh, aye. I don't know what his premiums were, but she scooped close to seven figures. Then poof,' she created a double fist with her hands and made then explode outwards, 'she vanishes with it.'

Big Ben asked, 'How do you know how much she got if you two didn't speak?'

'Because she bragged about it to Shelley McHugh. She even showed her the cheque when it came through the post. Shelley kept her secret until she realised her friend had absconded and didn't even pause to say goodbye. My brother's wife was a nasty piece of work. Wherever she is, I hope she's in pain.'

Steering away from her line of thought, I asked how about mementos. 'Do you have any photographs of your brother with his old friends from the SOS? You said they came here to visit.'

She shook her head, doing so as she was exhaling so a cloud of smoke shimmied into the air. I was trying not to cough as the air in the kitchen became less and less bearable. 'No. Pictures were taken though. Their last reunion was a big thing. It was a couple of years back now and they all brought their wives. I think even the ladies were quite close still. I went along with my two and Rob sorted out a big barbeque down by the water.'

'At the beach?' Big Ben wasn't sure which body of water she meant.

His question drew a laugh from her. 'Aye, you could call it a beach. It's not exactly Miami though. This is Scotland, pal. The water's cold enough to kill you.'

Interrupting her, I pursued the thing I wanted. 'You said pictures were taken. Where would I find copies of them, please?'

She curled her top lip. 'I suppose, if they exist still, they would be at the house. It's all digital now so they'd be on his computer. No. No, hold on. They did print some off. I remember seeing them.'

'But they would be at the house,' I clarified.

'If anywhere.' She stubbed out her cigarette.

Hopefully, Big Ben said, 'I don't suppose you have a key.'

Something to Hide

That she didn't have a key came as no surprise: it was a long shot. I needed to get into the house but decided to push on to Aberdeen first. We had to come back this way and I wanted it to be darker before we attempted to break in: we would do no one any favours getting arrested here.

The G Wagon's Satnav did its trick once more, tracking us north toward Aberdeen. It was a single road almost the whole way there, the A92 winding along the rugged coast-line through a lot of open land and not much else until it went through a village or a small town that were in the rear-view mirror mere moments after we reached them.

Aware of the time, because our flight was set for 1720hrs, we wanted to give ourselves as much breathing space as possible by going fast. However, the sixty-mile journey took ninety minutes, the average speed kept low by farm trucks, tractors, other lumbering large vehicles which were often difficult to get around, plus slowing down to obey speed signs in the small villages and towns.

By the time we reached the home of Mr and Mrs

Guthrie, parents to Greta Guthrie who grew up to marry a soldier, the clock on the dashboard showed a time of 1106hrs. We still had plenty of time, but no time to waste.

In the car, I called to check in with my parents, mercifully getting dad instead of mum who was in the smallest room, he said. They were fine, he assured me. Big Ben's television worked like any other television so mum wasn't missing her shows and she had her knitting bag with her like always. She'd made a sign to go on Big Ben's door which had stopped most of the female callers from bothering to knock. I dreaded to think what the sign might say and elected not to ask.

I'd next called Amanda who had left the penthouse suite to pursue a case. She promised she was being vigilant and that if she was being watched or tailed, they must be really good because she hadn't seen anyone. Strangely, it wasn't all that reassuring.

The Guthries lived in a small semi-detached house opposite a park with a lake. The lake had completely frozen, forcing the waterfowl to walk around on top as they looked forlornly through the ice. It was a pleasant area, and so much nicer for them to have a view of something other than a row of houses. However, it didn't look to be an affluent area. Glancing around, I spotted twenty-year-old Fords, battered French cars, and tired Skodas. Until I looked back at the Guthries' driveway. In front of their garage, a brand-new Mercedes glistened beneath its layer of snow.

The path to their door had been cleared, the shovel used for the task propped against the garage door as if the task were only recently completed. Big Ben got to the house first, knocking on the doorframe politely with his knuckles and stepping back to wait next to me.

A shadow moved inside and came nearer, forming the

silhouette of a woman as it neared the frosted glass of the front door. 'Mrs Guthrie?' I enquired as she opened the door.

'Err, yes,' she replied hesitantly like she didn't want to admit it in case I had a bill for her.

'I do hope you can spare us a moment of your time. It's about Greta.'

As always, my eyes were glued to hers to see what they would do. I expected excitement possibly, the anticipation that I might be here with news about her whereabouts. Or worry, because I might be here to tell her that her daughter's body had been found. I got neither thing. What I saw was a spike of panic.

'Can we come in, please,' said Big Ben, making a big show of being cold. 'We're from England and just not used to these temperatures.'

He ought to have got a smile at least, but she looked like she wanted to slam the door instead. I took a wild leap and said, 'We're not from the insurance firm.'

Her hand went to her heart and her feet backed away just a pace. Big Ben moved forward, picking up on my cue when he said, 'We were in the army with her husband, Bob.'

Acting like a rabbit trying to choose between being eaten by a fox or a hawk, she darted her head forward to look outside, swinging it left to right to see if any neighbours were watching. Then she ducked back inside and invited us in. 'Please,' was all she said as she stepped out of the way.

'Was there someone at the door, love? I'm just putting the kettle on.' A man's voice echoed through from somewhere deeper in the house as she closed the cold outside where it belonged.

Big Ben raised his voice. 'Two teas, please, Julie Andrews.'

A moment of stunned silence was followed by a man's head appearing around a door frame.

Mr and Mrs Guthrie were in their mid-sixties. They had the vibe of a couple who had worked for everything they had and were enjoying retirement. Dressed in newish clothes, they spent their money sensibly and never indulged. All the furnishings in view were in good condition, as was the décor and carpets, but none of it was high end or lavish. The car outside was out of place.

Mrs Guthrie said, 'Wait here, please,' and shuffled forward for a quiet word with her husband. She got close and whispered, his eyes widening.

The longer I gave them to think up lies, the better they would be able to cover the truth. We were inside now with the door closed and it was just us, so I dropped any pretence. 'My name is Tempest Michaels. I'm a private investigator hired to look into the recent death and subsequent sighting of a former colleague of your son-in-law. Your son-in-law has also been seen since his supposed car accident.' Mrs Guthrie rolled her eyes I noticed, 'and your daughter has vanished. Is that not the case?'

'You've been talking to that ridiculous sister of his, haven't you?' accused Mrs Guthrie. 'Robert died in a terrible accident and our daughter took herself away to rediscover herself. That's what she told us before she left. There's nothing sinister going on here, Mr Michaels.'

I didn't believe her. The confidence she now displayed was new and hadn't surfaced at any point until now. 'She paid for the Mercedes, yes?' I asked. 'It's easy for me to check so I wouldn't bother lying.' I was lying - I had no way of checking who paid for it.

They didn't know that though, and despite his wife's approach to the situation, Mr Guthrie wasn't quite so ready to bluff his way out. 'Yes,' he blurted.

'Gordon!' his wife squealed.

'Sorry, love.'

'Look,' I raised my hands in a display of surrender. 'I'm not here to cause any trouble. I'm not going to report you or anything like that. I do need to speak to your daughter though.' I didn't tell them that all the other wives had gone missing. 'Please give me her phone number so I can stop chasing after her and eliminate her from my enquiries.'

'We don't have a phone number for her,' sighed Mrs Guthrie, and finally it sounded like she was telling me the truth. Her shoulders slumped in defeat, and she seemed to deflate before my eyes. 'We don't know anything,' she admitted. Then she turned toward her husband and patted his chest tenderly. 'I think perhaps you should make those cups of tea now, Gordon.'

In their kitchen, Mr and Mrs Guthrie brought us to a small dining table set against a window that overlooked their garden. There was a hiatus while the kettle boiled and since they now wanted to lay out their story, I chose to hold fire on my questions.

'Here you go, gents,' Gordon set two cups of steaming tea on the table, then went back for his wife's and his own.

I locked eyes with Mrs Guthrie, hoping that I wouldn't have to do more than that to prompt her. She exchanged a glance with her husband, flicked her eyes down to her tea as she gathered her thoughts and then back up. 'She called us the day Robbie died. She was upset, of course, but there was something else, like she was scared. I didn't ask her about it at the time; it was all such a shock. She said she was going to come and live with us for a while. The house had too many memories, that was her reason; at least it was the one she gave us.'

Gordon reached out to take his wife's hand. 'We went to Barry straight away. We were in the car within the hour, but she was surprised to see us. She didn't seem as upset as I thought she ought to be. Upset yes, but like Vera said, Greta seemed more nervous than distraught. His funeral took place the following week, on a Thursday. It rained the whole time.'

I was beginning to wonder when they would tell me something pertinent. 'I need to speak with her,' I reminded them. 'It's important. Did you ask her what it was that she was nervous about?'

'We did,' said Mrs Guthrie. 'It was the day after we arrived at her house, but she dismissed the notion and said we were imagining things. We went home after the funeral was done. We're retired, but we still have a life, and she said she needed to get on with hers.' She stopped talking to take a sip of her tea, holding the cup on her lap with both hands to keep them still. 'She appeared with the car about two weeks later. She said it was a gift for us. We'd never had the money for a nice car. Or even a new car. She said we deserved it. It was nice having her here, of course, but I couldn't shift the idea that something else was amiss. I asked her about her job, and she said the firm were holding it for her. And I asked her about the house and her bills, and she said they were all being taken care of. They weren't though. We didn't know it at the time, but she was lying to us and had already closed the bank account her bills came out of.' She paused for some more tea, and I took a gulp of mine as well.

Gordon picked up the narrative while his wife drank her tea. 'Then one day she was gone. No warning, no words of farewell. She didn't even take her things. She was just gone. Even her phone is still here.'

'Her phone?' I echoed. 'May I see it?'

The couple exchanged a glance. 'I suppose so,' murmured Mrs Guthrie. 'I'm sorry we were off with you when you first arrived.'

'It's his sister, you see,' said Gordon. 'She called here a week after Greta vanished claiming Robbie was still alive and demanding to speak with our daughter. We never told her that she had gone away.'

'Did you report her missing?' asked Big Ben, a frown creasing his forehead.

'Yes, of course.' The reply came from Mrs Guthrie, but I wasn't sure I believed it. I'd been focused on her husband when she spoke and missed the facial cues that might have tipped me off. She snapped out her answer, the reply coming instantly and without thought as if she'd been waiting for the question. An unresolved missing person report would still be live, so we could check on her statement later.

I downed the rest of my tea and placed the mug back on its coaster. 'May I please see her phone and other possessions?'

The house had three bedrooms, two doubles and a single. Greta's belongings, of which there weren't many, were in a suitcase, in a wardrobe, and in the top drawer of a chest of drawers. With the couples' permission, I placed the suitcase on the bed and opened it. I was looking for the phone charger for a start, but also for anything else that might leap out as a clue.

Big Ben picked up the phone, which was lying on her nightstand. It was utterly dead; I hadn't even bothered to check. The charger was in the suitcase, lying on top of a pair of white denim jeans when I flipped the lid, but as I passed it to Big Ben, the familiar jangle of keys grabbed my attention. I almost upended the suitcase to find them but managed to resist; I was being watched by the missing woman's parents.

Carefully I rooted through the suitcase, taking things out as if they were treasured possessions and placing them carefully on the bed with my right hand. With my left, I used the flat of my palm to feel around until I located the keys, then I squashed them so they wouldn't make a sound and found a rolled-up pair of socks to hide them in.

Meanwhile, Big Ben got enough juice into the phone to bring it back to life. It went through a moment of set up, rebooting from being fully shut down, but the torrent of beeps from incoming messages, waiting in the ether to finally arrive weeks or months after they were sent, never arrived.

Frowning, I looked across at the screen. It displayed the manufacturers home screen, the one you get when you buy it and who doesn't customise their phone with a picture of something?

'It's been wiped,' said Big Ben. 'Greta must have performed a factory reset.'

Instantly, a question occurred which I didn't voice – How would she know to do that if she was grabbed against her will?

I moved in close to Big Ben so our shoulders were touching, and it looked like we were both staring at the phone screen. The arm touching his was behind my back, frantically stuffing the socks and keys into my back pocket. We faced the Guthries so they couldn't see the movement, and though I felt bad for stealing, I now also believed I had a way to get into her house that wouldn't get me arrested.

Clearly there was nothing to find on the phone and the ticking clock ticked louder with every passing minute. The rest of her possessions got nothing more than a cursory glance; there was nothing here. She brought clothing and makeup and very little else. She vanished out of the blue a few weeks after her husband and left everything she owned behind. It looked like an abduction.

Except … she took the time to wipe the memory on her phone first.

Wild Theories

They were hiding something, that much I felt certain of, but I suspected they were more worried about the insurance claim turning out to be fraudulent than they were anything else. I could feel a genuine concern for their daughter and whether she was safe, but I didn't think they had filed a missing person report and that struck me as odd too.

She was missing, but she took the time to wipe her phone as if she knew she were about to vanish. I thought all these things as Big Ben raced the Mercedes G Wagon south once more. I couldn't check the bunch of keys until we were in the car and away from the Guthries but just as I hoped, I had a bunch of keys for a house. I couldn't be certain it would open her house, but I figured the odds were on my side this time.

'I think she's with her husband,' said Big Ben, breaking the silence.

I pursed my lips and nodded. 'Me too. It's that or she is dead and someone else, someone she trusted, wiped the phone. If Rob McTavish has been killing his old team members, then he might just have killed his wife too. Fake his own death, wait for her to collect the life insurance, then kill her and abscond. Maybe she was in on it, but he double crossed her. Equally, maybe she is just as murderous as he.'

Big Ben took a deep and thoughtful breath, sucking it in through his nose and holding it as he worked the problem in his head. 'It has to be one or the other. Rob McTavish is still alive, and he's been killing his teammates. Staging their deaths to look like accidents.'

'You know this means he had to kill someone else to take his place. Someone had to be identified by his wife.'

'That's the other reason I think she is still alive. I think he depended on her for this to work. My only question is why he would do it now? Why now when he only had one man from the team left to kill? He could have faked his death at any point, but did he need to fake it at all? Each death is recorded as an accident which means there is no investigation. No one was looking to find out what happened to the first four team members. So why did he feel he needed to vanish?'

'Money,' I stated simply. 'The things we investigate are almost always to do with money or sex. He killed Dean Moore because he wanted to, but Dean's wife gets a fat cheque from a life insurance policy, so he kidnaps her and tortures her until she gives up the money. I believe he did the same to the other victims. The police will never look his way because he is dead. Maybe it was important that he didn't die first or last.'

'We can ask him when we find him,' growled Big Ben, flooring the accelerator to get around a tractor.

My phone pinged in my pocket and I lifted it out, absentmindedly expecting to find a message from Jane,

Amanda, or my mum. It was none of those. The message was from the Undead.

'You chose the wrong path. Did you think we wouldn't know that you chose to meddle? We are the Undead, we see everything. We see when the living buy tickets for a flight to Scotland. We see the secure community your family are hiding in. We are no longer interested in them; they were just a way to make you see sense. Now it is too late, and you know the truth. For that, you must die.'

I read the message aloud for Big Ben and got to watch as he tightened his grip on the steering wheel in anger. 'What truth?' he snarled. 'That Rob McTavish faked his own death? It's not like we have any hard evidence.'

'They must think that we do. We triggered something when we came here. Maybe there was someone here with a number to call. Maybe they were watching us and followed us to the airport.'

'Maybe they've bugged my apartment,' suggested Big Ben. 'I have women in and out of there all the time. I often don't learn their names. It's bad to admit it now, truthfully it only just occurred to me, but it wouldn't be hard for them to find a lady willing to visit me and put bugs around the place when I take a shower.'

'We'll have to scan for them.' I called Jane.

She answered before it had a chance to ring. 'Tempest, how's it going?'

'Rob McTavish faked his death; we're fairly sure of that. Then he either murdered his wife, or she was in on the whole thing and is with him now. I think ...'

'Hold on,' she interrupted me. 'Amanda is here and so are your parents. I'm putting you on speakerphone.'

'Hi, guys,' said Amanda.

Next dad spoke, 'Kiddo. You men having any luck getting to the bottom of this nonsense?'

Finally, mum's voice came over the airwaves. 'I hope you are both behaving yourselves.'

I rolled my eyes and repeated my line about Rob McTavish. 'Amanda, can you tap into your old friends at the station and see if a missing person report was ever filed for Greta McTavish? She wiped her phone before she went missing. That's not a normal thing to do.' A strange sniffing noise came through the speaker. 'What's that?' I asked.

Dad said, 'Sorry, that's just Dozer. I put him on the counter, and he can hear your voice. He's sniffing the phone and looking at it with his head cocked to one side.' I could picture my daft dog doing just that.

'I'll get right on it,' said Amanda. 'Anything else?'

'Yeah. Can you scan Big Ben's place for bugs?'

Jane gasped. 'You think they might be listening in?'

'They knew we went to Scotland somehow. They seem to know what we are doing. Checking will tell us one way or the other.'

'I can do that,' said Amanda.

I wiggled my jaw around as I thought about whether I wanted Jane to focus on the wives. It seemed like we were clutching at straws already, though our visit to Scotland hadn't been without progress. 'Jane, can you have another go at investigating the wives?'

'What do you want me to find on them specifically?' asked Jane.

'They are vanished, it would seem, but how many of them displayed behaviour that makes it look like they knew they were going to vanish? Did they quit their jobs or just stop showing up? Did they visit relatives in the last days before they vanished?'

Big Ben cut in. 'You think Greta went to her parents to say goodbye?'

'It's just one theory. It could be nothing but chance that took her there and her husband could have killed her and wiped her phone.' I gave the listeners a scenario. 'He fakes his death with his wife's help. Greta identifies his body, but it could be anyone. He's killed a man and put him in the driver's seat with identification on him that says he's Rob McTavish. Provided he had facial injuries, they'll never know. All Greta has to do is sob uncontrollably and say it's her husband. No one will question her. She then claims the life insurance, getting a big pay out with a plan to rendezvous when it is safe. Rob McTavish has a different plan though. He watches her parents' place, waits for them to go out and goes to his wife. She's expecting him, but he kills her, wipes her phone and removes the body leaving all her possessions behind.'

'That's pretty cold,' said dad.

'They are trained killers,' I reminded him. 'It's still pretty cold, but I think this goes back to whatever happened in Iraq. That secret has festered away inside Rob's gut. Four years ago, he killed Andrew Kemp and then had to make Kemp's wife disappear. Something must have triggered him. It would have been bottled up all this time, but Kemp says something or does something that pushes McTavish over the edge. Once he kills the first one, the flood gate opens, and he slowly works his way through all of them. Maybe he finds a way to get his hands on their money by accident, maybe that was always part of the plan. Either way, he doesn't want to get caught so he fakes his own death.'

'That's a solid scenario,' agreed Amanda supportively. 'A dozen other scenarios could be made to fit also. We need to scare up some proof quickly.'

Jane asked, 'How do we find out what their big secret is? If this all goes back to an event in Iraq – you said there was a big investigation at the time – then who can shed some light on it?'

I huffed out a breath. Finding out was something I desperately wanted to know at the time. The questions, the three-on-one interviews with special investigators demanding we tell them what we saw and what we heard went on for months after the war. It tainted the whole experience and made me feel dirty. Did anyone know anything? I certainly didn't.

'We would have to find their old commanding officer,' I replied around a beaten sigh. 'I don't even remember his name.'

'We called him Spanky Monkey,' Big Ben chipped in with a smile. 'He had a double-barrelled name that sounded something like that.'

I snorted a laugh as I remembered too. 'That's right. Look, his name won't be hard to find. However, I doubt he will talk even if he knows anything, which he might not. I think Dean's team did something terrible but got away with it because they were the only ones there. It happened when they were together as a team and they stuck together to deny it. Only, maybe Rob wasn't part of it and couldn't handle the shame that went with keeping their secret. Maybe it wasn't just him and he has a partner. We still have far more questions than answers.'

Changing the subject, Amanda asked, 'Are you on your way back here?'

'Yes, babe. We need to make one stop on our way to the airport, but we'll be back in time for dinner. Then maybe we can start to thrash out how to find Rob McTavish.'

I could almost hear the frown in her voice when my mother asked, 'Where do you need to stop off?'

In and Out

Going up the McTavish's garden path, we chatted amiably to give anyone watching the impression we ought to be there. We looked relaxed and we had a key. Furtive movements would have been picked up and possibly reported to the police. The sun was beginning to dip, though it hadn't made it all that far above the horizon at any point. Yet it was still light and the snow on the ground amplified what light there was.

Greta's bunch contained half a dozen keys, but only one I thought likely to be for the front door. Making a show of selecting it, I said a silent prayer as I pushed it into the keyhole. It slid in with no resistance, turned, and we were inside.

I gave myself a mental high-five as I stepped over the mound of mail.

'That's a lot of final notice warnings,' observed Big Ben, looking down at several envelopes that stuck out starkly because of the big red letters on them. Half the pile had to be pizza flyers and other junk. There were several free newspapers among the letters, and a Sunseeker yacht catalogue making the pile all the thicker. The mail held no interest.

'Split up?' suggested Big Ben as he slipped on a pair of latex gloves.

I nodded, 'I'll take downstairs.' A small hallway linked the front door with the rest of the house and the upper floor via a staircase. Big Ben's heavy footsteps reached the upper hallway, where, in the silence of the house, I could track his every movement.

Rob McTavish hadn't gone on to make a lot of money when he left the army, but their furniture and household items were in nearly new condition, so he wasn't hurting for money either. It wasn't a big house, but that didn't mean there weren't still lots of places to hide things. Wearing my own set of gloves to avoid leaving prints, and taking a methodical approach, I started in their kitchen. Going cupboard to cupboard, drawer to drawer, I looked for anything that might yield a clue.

I wanted to find a bank account login and their insurance paperwork which might show how much had been paid out and when. Or it might show when the policy was taken out or if the insured sum was recently changed – a possible sign they were planning his disappearance. I also wanted to find the photographs his sister spoke of. Pictures from a reunion might show me nothing or might show me something vital.

The kitchen revealed nothing much of value but looking in the fridge with my breath held in case there were horrors inside, I found it to be clean and almost empty. I'd expected there to be a half-drunk carton of milk from six months ago but laughed at myself when I remembered that Greta had knowingly moved out to go to her parents.

The rest of the downstairs was a lounge/diner. At some point, a wall had been knocked through, making two rooms into one. It gave the house better flow, but also exposed how small it was. What I didn't see anywhere was a computer. There was no desk for one and no space where one might have sat. Hoping Big Ben had found it upstairs, I continued my search. I found old CDs in a cupboard, I found money down the back of their couch, and I found where they had moved a rug to hide a red wine stain. I did not, however, find any incriminating evidence which revealed the nature of the crime in Iraq or anything related to my investigation.

A knock at the front door gave me a start, my heart beating out a staccato rhythm as the sound broke the silence without warning. Big Ben had been moving around above me, but I heard him freeze too. Ignoring it wasn't going to work, so I called out, 'I'll get it!' and pulled off my gloves.

At the door, I moved the pile of mail to one side with my left foot, fixed a congenial smile, and opened it to see who was outside.

The first thing I noticed was that it had started snowing again and it was coming down hard. In the twenty minutes we'd been inside, the sun's path toward the horizon had continued unabated and the streetlamps were now lit. Snow whirled around them, flakes shining brightly for a flash and then disappearing, only to be replaced by the next ones.

On the doorstep, six inches lower than the floor on which I stood, was a man in his sixties. He had a stern expression and he didn't say anything, so I did. 'Hi. Are you our neighbour? We just bought the place from the bank. It's all a bit odd finding someone else's belongings here. We can't move in yet, but we thought we'd have a look around.'

I stuck out my hand, 'I'm George.' I wasn't giving him my real name.

He looked down at my hand and back up at my face, but he didn't move his own hand to take mine. 'The house isn't for sale,' he stated. 'How did you come to buy it?' It was an open accusation. I hadn't readied myself to defend our actions, and when I hesitated instead of answering or arguing, he turned away. 'I'm calling the police,' he snapped at me.

I slammed the door shut. 'Ben! We're going to have company!'

His voice echoed back down the stairs, 'Roger. Did you find anything?'

'Not a thing. Did you find a computer?'

To answer my question, fast moving feet brought him to the top of the stairs. He had things stuffed in his coat. It was half unzipped to act as a giant pocket where pieces of paper, what looked like envelopes, and plastic wallets – the type one uses in a folder to protect the paper within – were all attempting to spill back out and escape. In his arms he carried a computer tower.

'I didn't have time to get it working, but I found their home office and ransacked it. We can see whether this contains treasures or is also wiped clean when we get back to my place.'

'Brilliant.' I wanted to search for longer, but the police showing up would add a level of complication we didn't need. This was the best we could hope for. 'Let's go.'

And go we did. The contents of his coat were spilled on the backseat along with the tower itself. The neighbour ran after us, trying to get a picture of the number plate on the back of the car and shouting insults and threats as Big Ben gunned the engine and slewed the back wheels through the snow to escape.

It was a straight shot to the airport; our eyes peeled the whole way for squad cars looking our way. The Mercedes G Wagon wasn't an everyday car, which is to say it is easy to spot if someone is looking for it. There were some tense moments when we reached the airport and had to drive by several police cars with the cops sat idly inside, but either the neighbour hadn't been able to get our plate or never made the call. Whichever the case, we got away clean, returning the car, asking the chap at the rental unit for a carrier bag into which we dumped all the looted mail and paperwork, and finding our way to check-in.

At the counter, a thought occurred to me. 'I didn't find passports.' I got a raised eyebrow from Big Ben. 'At their house. I searched downstairs quite thoroughly, and I didn't find passports.'

He got what I was saying. 'I didn't either and I think they would have been in the office with everything else. They were quite organised. Of course, they might just not have passports. Some people don't.'

'Or they took them,' I suggested.

'But if he's faked his own death and she's registered as a missing person, surely they wouldn't risk using them to board a flight.'

I pursed my lips. 'What about a ferry crossing? To get out of the country they would check the passport, but I don't think it's the same stringent system. I'm not even sure they check them at all.'

He shrugged. 'It's just another little clue that we could choose to reinforce our argument that they are alive and killing the other team members. Or it could be nothing.'

He was right. We had to be watchful that we didn't build a false picture from the clues we found.

The queue moved forward, and it was our turn, a short, plain woman at the check-in desk waving us forward. Her badge gave her name as Louise.

'Good afternoon, Louise. How is your day so far?' I asked her, handing over our tickets.

I got a professional smile from her as she performed her job in a gleeless manner. 'Any bags to check?' she asked.

'No. Just carry on today.'

She looked up at me and to the computer tower in my hands. 'You can't take that on board. You'll have to check it.'

'That won't do it any good. It's too delicate to go in the hold,' I argued.

I got a blank look from her which lasted for a two count before she repeated herself. 'You can't take that on board. You'll have to check it.'

Big Ben nudged me to the side. 'Let me try mine,' he murmured as he took my place in front of Louise. Sidelined, I took a step back and watched as he leaned forward at the waist and hit her with his smouldering gaze. He didn't say anything, he just held the gaze on her until her lips parted and she began to pant slightly.

Sixty seconds later, we had our boarding passes and were heading through security. I still had the computer tower in my arms because, when Big Ben asked, it was fine to take it on board. Louise stamped our boarding passes, missing twice as she wasn't looking at what she was doing and giggled with embarrassment when Big Ben leaned forward another foot to kiss her cheek and whisper something in her ear that made her pupils dilate.

There were many occasions when I loathed him. This

wasn't one of them because for once he used his magic for good.

I relaxed on the flight and let myself have a rum and coke. Big Ben had one too and we toasted making it this far. It was part joke and part not. The man we believed we were up against was capable, well-trained, and motivated – he was already dead and wanted to stay that way. I held no doubt that he would kill us to keep his secret.

Until the rum hit my bloodstream and I sagged into my chair, I hadn't realised quite how tense I felt. The messages from the Undead always referred to plural persons. More than one, at least, which could be a clever bluff, or might be the truth. We still didn't know who or what we were up against. If it wasn't Rob McTavish, then we were in even deeper trouble than I believed, and we'd been following a false trail.

That they could be anywhere, troubled me deeply and as we filtered back through Stansted airport and into the arrivals lounge, my eyes darted everywhere, looking at men and women alike. Rob could be disguised as an old man, his wife could be here looking right at me, and I would never know.

Despite my fears, we arrived back at the Lotus unmolested. I passed Big Ben the computer tower at that point so I could check the car over. It harked back to operations in places like Northern Ireland where a favoured method of the various terrorist groups was to fit a bomb on a car. Detonation could be remote using a phone, automatic by use of a tilt switch, or one of a dozen other methods, all of which would generate the same instantly deadly result. They were easy to fit too.

A quick inspection of the undercarriage and wheel arches reassured me, but it wasn't until we were a mile down the road that I took my next breath. We were maintaining a level of vigilance that was exhausting, and we had to have eyes everywhere.

If I had known I had no reason to worry about my car and the drive home, I would have driven a lot faster. They weren't targeting me, and I should have anticipated that. They were going for the soft target.

A Well Executed Assault

The explosion shocked me. Making my hands twitch the steering wheel to almost send it into the wall that borders the river. We had left the motorway and were coming into Maidstone along Royal Engineers Road. Where the road meets the river in the centre of town, Big Ben's gated community sits on the other side of the water, and we were level with it when the fireball lit the sky.

There was no snow here, not yet at least, though the temperature had dropped to below freezing and there were dark clouds everywhere. I saw the clouds because the orange flame reflected off them to throw light back down on the area below.

Big Ben shouted, 'Go!' and go I did, slamming the gear stick back down into second and flooring the accelerator. I had to weave between the slow-moving evening traffic of late-night Christmas shoppers and people out for dinner, and I jumped first one red light, then another, then changed lanes and drove against the traffic. Maidstone town centre is a big one-way system with two bridges across the river. They form a giant roundabout which I had to fight against, opposing the flow as I tried to get to Big Ben's place.

While I drove like a maniac, Big Ben phoned Amanda.

I heard her panicked voice answer, 'Ben! There was an explosion outside! Where are you guys?'

'We're sixty seconds away. We saw the fireball! Get out of the suite now!'

'We're already going!' she shouted back.

The car clanged painfully as I mounted the pavement to get around queuing cars and suddenly there were flashing lights and a wailing siren in my rear-view as a cop car tried to fight its way through the traffic after me.

The cops were giving chase, but I wanted them on my tail for what was to come.

Bursting free of the traffic as I jumped yet another red light, I hit the gas again to push the car to a suicidal speed as we closed with his building. I had to crush the brake pedal to slow the Lotus as we neared his turning and used the handbrake to coax the car's rear end around.

There was a thick veil of smoke loitering around the gates and we both knew what caused it: smoke grenades. This was a planned assault.

The barrier pole was lying to one side and bent in the middle. The guard hut, put there so the person manning the gate could keep out of the weather and have somewhere to put a drink or a snack, had been blown to smithereens. If I had to guess, I would say a rocket propelled grenade had been used. Of the guard, I could see no sign, and that didn't bode well for him. His health was not my dominant concern right now, getting my family, my girlfriend, my dogs, and my colleagues out of this was. To do that, required knowingly running into battle unarmed against an unknown number of assailants who had already demonstrated that they were armed.

The car powered through the gate, bouncing over the fallen barrier pole at which point I slammed on the brakes again, and we bailed out. A shout from inside the building drew my attention. The lower floors were all but invisible through the smoke which was working for us as much as it was against: we couldn't see if there was an armed force ahead of us, but they couldn't see us either.

In the road, the wailing police siren heralded their arrival, but they didn't follow us into the property. Perhaps the swirling smoke kept them at bay, but from inside the building, the crack of shots punctuated the chill night air giving the police officers no choice but to react.

We were running for the main entrance, keeping low and always looking for cover. More shots rang out, these ones coming from above us and inside the building. It sounded like more than one weapon, but the shooter or shooters were being conservative with the ammunition; selecting single shot not burst.

Big Ben and I slammed into the front wall of his building, finding the front door only because we knew roughly where it ought to be. Taking a moment to assess, the strobe lights from the police car lit the smoke eerily. I could hear the adrenalin in the officers' voices as they called for back-up and advised dispatch they were proceeding inside. There were shots fired, one shouted into his radio. They were armed only with a baton each, but it was still their job to protect the public. Back up would get here quickly, but not quickly enough to prevent a massacre inside the building if the gunmen found who they were after: i.e. my family and friends.

With two fingers, Big Ben pointed to the door. He was

going in. I should cover him, but what with? I was armed with sassy wit and a good after-dinner conversation, hardly effective tools in a firefight. If we came up against any armed women, Big Ben could always make their knickers fall off - that ought to distract them, but the truth was that the only play I had was to give the attackers what they wanted: me.

I opened the door with an angry kick. 'McTavish!' I shouted. 'McTavish. You want me? I'm outside.' Running into the building and certain death made no sense. If I could draw him or them outside, I would get them away from the residents inside, including Amanda, Jane, and my parents, plus I might stand a chance of evading them until an armed police unit arrived.

Slamming into the wall next to me, a cop appeared. 'Tempest?'

I turned to find it was Brad Hardacre, a former colleague of Amanda's. He and I didn't exactly like each other, but this wasn't the time for that.

I leaned inside the building again. 'McTavish, you utter coward. I'm going to bring this whole thing down on you. I just had a look around your house in Barry. I know about Iraq. I know why you are doing this. I'm going to blow the lid off the whole thing. The dead will not be able to stay dead soon.' I was goading him, and I was lying. I hadn't got a damned clue why he faked his own death, but he couldn't know that.

A volley of shots tore into the stairs to let me know I had his attention. They had been fired downward from a floor somewhere above. 'You know nothing, Tempest Michaels,' replied an assured voice. 'Your foolish bluff reveals how ill-informed you are.' The voice had a trace of humour to it.

He'd been concerned I knew more than I did, and I had just tipped my hand by guessing wrong.

The wail of sirens screaming through Maidstone gave me a new line to try. 'Armed police are coming, McTavish. Do you think you can escape once they arrive? Do you want a hostage situation? No one ever wins those. We are at the front entrance. There are police here with us. Give yourself up!'

It was hopeful to say the least, and the mocking voice echoing back down found me amusing. 'You will never see us coming, Tempest Michaels. We are Undead Incorporated, and you never stood a chance.' His response came with a fresh volley of bullets which chewed up the floor at the base of the stairs a little more, then a familiar bouncing tin can sound told me grenades were coming down the stairs.

I grabbed Brad's shoulders, just as Big Ben – standing the other side of the entrance – ducked the other way taking Brad's partner with him. The plinking, plonking noise came closer, but no explosion ripped the front doors from their mounts and showered us with glass. The grenades were yet more smoke.

The police arrived in force in the next moment, the smoke from earlier now dissipated by the wind to give them a clear view of the building. Armed officers swarmed the grounds, bellowed commands bringing them forward in teams with their weapons up. We were far from safe still, but with Brad to escort me, I could at least avoid being one of those they assume might be a target for once.

I hunkered close to the building as it gave protection on one flank, and from there, I called Amanda.

'Is it over?' she begged, her breathing fast and hard.

'Maybe. Armed police are about to storm the building. Where are you?'

She took a deep breath to steady herself. 'We're on the roof. I think they went into Big Ben's place. We heard explosions and shots, but we got away clean. They were on the stairs, cutting off our escape, so we went up.'

Brad could hear our conversation and was relaying it via his radio to the armed police now inside. We could also hear the police shouting back and forth inside the building as they worked their way cautiously upward. They were covering all avenues of escape, and though we waited for the inevitable clash, no shots were fired. A tense few minutes stretched out as I waited for the police to corner McTavish and whoever was with him. I waited and waited, and it became apparent that I would wait forever because, like any well executed assault, they had an escape plan.

McTavish was gone, but he'd answered me, and I could at least rejoice that I was closing in.

That was when it hit me.

'Ben,' I called to get his attention. 'Did you notice anything about his accent?'

He nodded, a look of concern on his face. 'Yeah. Whoever you were speaking to wasn't Scottish.'

Destruction

The shouting inside the building continued for some time as the police went through it apartment by apartment, clearing each domicile to be certain the gunmen weren't hiding inside with a family as their hostages. It took a lot of men and a lot of coordination to organise because they wanted the families to stay put in their homes, not flee from the building, which is what a lot of the families were trying to do.

Waiting around, I made a phone call to someone I thought I could rely on and someone I hoped the Undead would not be watching or expecting. My judgement that they wouldn't attack Big Ben's place had been way off the mark and resulted in dozens of people being terrorised by tonight's assault. We wouldn't be able to stay at Big Ben's place. Even if it wasn't utterly destroyed, which Amanda made it sound like it was, remaining there just invited another attack and I couldn't allow the residents here to be placed in danger again.

The Undead would come for me again, that much I felt

certain of, and next time, I needed to be able to control it. I didn't know much about the place we were going to next, but what little I did know led me to believe it was the right place to go. I wasn't going to discuss it with anyone yet. I was going to get everyone to safety and see what happened.

I had a blanket around my shoulders to keep the cold at bay – a police officer I didn't know brought it to me because there was nowhere warm to go, but as things settled down and the police declared the building clear, I spotted Chief Inspector Quinn taking command. He wasn't the leader of the armed response unit which meant he'd been forced to wait until they were satisfied the armed threat was gone before he could take charge. Now holding the reins, he deployed his officers, and he wanted to know what was going on.

Unsurprisingly, he made a beeline for me. 'Mr Michaels, would you care to explain?'

Big Ben got in first, and typically for him, he wasn't very helpful. 'Yeah, I can explain, Quinny. You're terrible at your job and never listen when we tell you there's about to be a war.'

'We didn't tell him,' I whispered loud enough for Quinn to hear since I thought it was a fairly pertinent point.

'Then his detectives suck at their jobs,' argued Big Ben. 'There are dead people shooting up the place and kidnapping women. Also, a dickhead with a ponytail trashed my car and I can't get it fixed because it's stuck on the driveway of a woman who has most likely been kidnapped and may right now be lying in a shallow grave. Your response to the missing person report might need to be stepped up a notch.'

CI Quinn had no idea what Big Ben was talking about, of course, because the missing person report had been logged in Swanley. Nevertheless, I helped to fill in few blanks. 'My client vanished from her house about thirty-six hours ago. We were there with her, but a known local hoodlum arrived, took a bat to my colleague's car, and in the affray that followed, Mrs Moore went missing. It follows a pattern that leads me to believe she has been murdered. This is going to take a while to explain, and I would like to find my parents since they were the targets tonight.'

I got a raised eyebrow. 'They were the targets? Is it the same person or persons who drugged them two nights ago?'

'They were drugged then?' I sought to confirm.

'Indeed. I got the report back from the crime lab this evening. They identified the substance used as Salvia divinorum. It's not native to this country and is illegal to import in an aerosol form because it is a weaponised hallucinogen. Its effects are short term, but instant, as I understand it. The person employing it would only need to use suggestion to create the leap from reality to fantasy. Prolonged use is very dangerous – the plant is highly toxic – but in small doses, your parents should suffer no long-term ill effects. It brings me neatly back to tonight's events, Mr Michaels. Gun fights in Maidstone are so rare that there has never been one before. This is a first.'

I corrected him. 'Technically, it wasn't a gun fight, because only one side had guns. All we had to hit them with were insults.'

'Nevertheless, Mr Michaels. You want my attention, now you have it. I need to know what you know and fast.' The first thought to enter my head was that his head would probably explode if he knew what I knew. 'Perhaps we should go to Mr Winters' apartment,' Quinn suggested.

'Penthouse suite,' Big Ben corrected him needlessly.

I called Amanda and let her know we would meet them there. 'We're already inside,' she told me. 'It got too cold on the roof and when we met officers on the stairs, they insisted we return to our property. You may need to tell Big Ben to brace himself.'

Her warning failed to capture the level of destruction that faced us when we walked through his front door. In fact, I need to correct that statement because we needed to step over what was left of his front door. They had used an exploding shotgun shell, or something similar, to gain entry, destroying a good portion of the door in the process.

Big Ben took a moment to pause and look around. His front door opened to a lobby which joined the centre hub of the suite on the left. To the right was a toilet which they had also put an exploding round through to make sure anyone in it was paying attention. Then, it appeared they stopped to throw grenades into the centre hub where his lounge area, dining room, and open plan kitchen could be found. The grenades hadn't found any human targets, but everything else was beyond repair.

As we stepped inside, Bull barked. He was happy to see me, as was his brother, Dozer, both dogs squirming in my dad's arms as they tried to get free. Dad clung on to them because the floor was littered with shards of glass from the television, parts of the marble kitchen counter, and tiny fragments of shrapnel from the grenades. I went to them, sweeping the debris from the kitchen counter with one arm so dad could put the dogs down.

'I needed to redecorate anyway,' muttered Big Ben as he surveyed his home. 'I hope my insurance has a dead person attack clause.'

While my friend bit down his anger and disappointment, CI Quinn moved to the breakfast bar where he checked my parents, Amanda, and Jane were in one piece. Even Amanda chose to give him a polite response. I gave her a hug, and then one for my mother too, but she was drinking wine directly from the bottle and shrugged me off because she needed her hands free.

'She's just a little shaken,' my father assured me. I didn't doubt it for a second.

'Dead people,' CI Quinn echoed. 'I think it's time I listened to what you have to say.'

Before I gave him any information, I turned to Amanda. 'Did you get a feel for how many there were?' I asked.

She shook her head. 'We didn't see them,' then she considered her claim. 'Actually, it had to be at least two teams. We could hear them destroying this place, but going up the stairs, there was someone coming up it and there were at least two set of footsteps.'

'I think it was two,' agreed my father. 'There had to be at least four people if we add them together.'

'How many stairwells are there?' I posed my question to Big Ben.

'Two plus the elevators.'

If I were coming in, I would want to cover both stairwells. 'At least four people, possibly more.' I let that hit my brain. I had been completely wrong with my theory about Rob McTavish acting alone. What did it mean though? Had he recruited others? Had another member of the same team also faked his death?

'Mr Michaels?' CI Quinn prompted me. Everyone was looking my way as they waited for me to explain things. Except mum. Mum was rummaging in the pock-marked refrigerator for more wine.

I blew out a breath and leaned wearily on the kitchen counter. With my thoughts gathered, I did my best to tell the chief inspector, and the half dozen other officers listening in, all about Dean Moore and his team, about the

event in Iraq which I suspected was the root cause or cata-
lyst behind the recent occurrences, and laid out what we
knew so far.

The police listened patiently until I ran out of words,
only then asking questions and seeking clarification.

The chief Inspector summed things up. 'You believe a
man called Rob McTavish faked his own death, had his wife
identify the body and claim his life insurance policy, and
that he, or they, are engaged in killing other members of a
special forces team who were possibly involved but never
convicted of a scandal in Iraq during or immediately after
the war in 2003?'

'That's what I did believe. Now I think I might have the
whole thing wrong. The man I exchanged words with wasn't
Scottish. I don't think it was Rob McTavish, which means
he has recruited someone else to his cause or there is
another member of the team still alive.'

'How sure are you that this is about whatever happened
in Iraq?' Quinn asked.

I gave him a sad laugh. 'I have no idea what this is
about. Not really. Two days ago, I was approached by a
widow who told me she was convinced her dead husband
was following her around. I was supposed to find out what
was going on. I picked up a tail in minutes, got threatened
directly within hours, and have been chasing my own tail
ever since. Whatever I have stumbled across, it's big enough
to kill for and my client might already be dead.'

'Okay.' The chief inspector had a determined look on
his face when he started handing out instructions to his officers. I knew him to be career orientated, and I didn't see it
as a good thing, but it did give him the drive to get the job
done. He recognised that this was front page stuff. The anti-
terror squad were coming and with them would be the

press; that was where CI Quinn wanted to shine. He would throw resources at this case, but that meant he was demanding we give him everything we had researched and discovered already. He would play hardball to get it if we didn't give it up willingly, and right was on his side. That was why I kept quiet about going to Rob McTavish's house and about the computer in the boot of my car. If I found anything I thought would help him, I would share it. Until then, I was going to keep it to myself. I did, however, show him the messages on my phone.

He read them with interest, then clicked his finger to summon a junior officer. 'Get me one of the boffins,' he ordered. 'I want to know everything there is to know about the phone that sent these messages.' I handed my phone over so they could make note of the Undead's number and forward the messages to another phone where they would be dissected. Chief Inspector Quinn looked around the room at my friends and family. 'I want to put you all into protective custody,' he announced as his officers busied themselves.

I gave him a flat, 'No,' in reply. 'We have a place to go. It is well away from anyone else, and the Undead will not think to look for us there.'

'Where?' he demanded to know.

I gave him a wry grin. 'No. If no one knows, no one can slip up.'

'Where are you taking us this time?' Amanda whispered in my ear, moving in close so no one else would hear.

'I'll show you,' I murmured back with a kiss to her cheek.

Mystery Destination

I had never been where we were going and so one might question my sanity for choosing to go there. It wasn't as bonkers as it might seem though. What I knew from my earlier phone call was that it was away from the towns and not even part of a village per se. It sat apart, and it was a recent acquisition. So recent, in fact that the owner was still unpacking, a task I proposed to help with.

I didn't cover up the fact that we were on the run from armed adversaries, nor did I hide that I was bringing parents, dogs, colleagues, and problems, but I did promise to help unpack and that did the trick.

My phone rang in the car. Since my Porsche was yet to be returned from the shop and Big Ben's car was still trapped at Mrs Moore's place, we were in the Lotus and it didn't have hands free equipment, so it was Big Ben who answered. Cramped into the passenger seat, his right shoulder touching my left as his bulk took up sixty percent of the available space, he thumbed the button and said, 'Hello, Amanda,'

'Tempest,' she replied, ignoring that it was Big Ben who addressed her. 'Where on Earth are you taking us?'

'To a friend's house,' I reassured her not for the first time.

We had a procession of cars winding through the country lanes as we left civilisation behind. We were out on the Hoo Peninsula where villages became more and more spread out. Allhallows on the coast was directly ahead of us, but we were going to stop short of that.

'Is it much further?' begged Jane, the passenger in Amanda's Mini. They were at the back with my parents in their Ford Escort sandwiched in between. Dad was driving because he was sober and mum was not, but his night vision is terrible, so we were going slow and being wary because the temperature was below freezing. This far off the beaten path, gritting trucks were unlikely.

'Your phone says to turn here,' Big Ben pointed out. The Lotus didn't come with Satnav either and phone signal was patchy, but I knew roughly where we were going.

To Amanda and Jane, I said, 'It's less than a mile now.'

It was even less than that, it turned out, and a silhouette framed in the doorway of a large and dark gothic house let me know the owner had seen us coming.

'Is that Frank?' asked Amanda.

I didn't need to answer because everyone could see him. The outside lights came on as he stepped out of the house, illuminating his scrawny frame and friendly face. He was a comic bookshop owner, but also an internet entrepreneur who was making a surprising amount of money. Five years ago, he'd been living in his mum's back bedroom. Now he owned a folly in the countryside. It boasted eleven bedrooms and a turret, plus, Frank assured me, passages, and rooms he hadn't yet found, and even a cellar he referred to as the dungeon.

I pulled just past him but chucked a wave so he would know it was me in the unfamiliar car. When I stopped, my parents came alongside, and Amanda parked right next to Frank. The snow was beginning to fall, an unusual occurrence in our part of the world where a few flakes may fall every few years, but a proper snowfall comes less than once a decade. This had the look and feel of the latter.

'Hi, everyone,' said Frank, smiling like he'd won the lottery. 'You're my first guests. There's a warm fire inside and a bottle of brandy warming next to it if you would like a nightcap.'

My mother barged her way to the front, her elbow in my ribs no accident as she responded to Frank's invitation. 'Is it good brandy?' she asked suspiciously. Not that she hung around to hear his answer; she was through the door and looking for the fire before the rest of us had a chance to greet our host.

'This is quite the place,' said Amanda, giving the much smaller man a hug.

'It was cheap too,' he chuckled, 'On account of its haunted nature. I got rid of the ghosts, or rather banished them to a single room with some ghost powder and protective circles when I moved in. I will find out if they are malevolent or not when I have a little more time.'

Leaning in behind Amanda so my lips were almost in her hair, I whispered, 'We'll be safe here.'

Mum was long gone, but the rest of us, with Frank's help, unloaded the cars and got everything inside. It helped that we had spent such a short time at Big Ben's because most of our belongings were still in bags.

Inside, with the giant oak door bolted behind us and the

cold locked outside, Frank led us to the room he was using to live in. 'It's been empty for years,' he explained. 'Since 1984, in fact, so I have quite a bit of updating to do. A new router, satellite and cabling to every room has been added, so all your devices should work.'

Ready to honour my promise to help him unpack, and despite the fatigue I felt from the last couple of days, I asked, 'What can we help you with?'

He waved an arm at me. 'Tempest, you are all my guests. There's no need to be helping me with anything.' Then a cheeky grin stole across his face. 'Would you like to see the dungeon? I've been setting up my weapon collection.'

Jane cocked a delicate eyebrow at him. 'Dungeon?'

Dungeon

I hadn't thought he was joking, but his boast about having a dungeon didn't prepare me for what he had to show us. Down a wide set of stone stairs, we descended into the Earth and the temperature rose noticeably as we reached the lowest level of his house.

'I'm still exploring' he explained. 'There are no plans for the house, but I found one staircase behind a moving wall panel already. It links the upper and lower floors where it exits in the larder by the kitchen.' He was gushing with excitement like a giddy schoolboy as he talked about the features of his ridiculous house. 'It was built in 1634 by Lord Huntingdon. He became a public victim of the civil war when his family were all put to death in the grounds of the house. I think one of the ghosts haunting this place might be his, actually.'

I kept quiet, unwilling to tell my host that he was mad since I'd done it so many times in the past already.

'I had some tradesmen in today to fit out the inside of my weapon room,' he explained. 'Not that I am sure how much use it will get now that the Kent League of Demonologists have disbanded.' The dungeon had that damp stone smell I associated with cellars, but the walls, when I touched them, were completely dry, as was the floor. I expected to find a layer of dust yet there was little of it underfoot. In every direction, lighting, some of it recently fitted, hung from the ceiling as white cables to connect them looped and snaked around. The modern lighting looked odd against the round stone pillars supporting the building. Each was made from six eighteen-inch-deep round blocks with arches at the top to spread the load. The distance, floor to ceiling had to be close to twelve feet, giving his cellar a sense of enormous space. He led us around a corner where, unexpectedly, we were facing a pair of modern steel doors. Inset to the righthand door was a digital palm reader.

Frank waggled his eyebrows, showing off, and with his right palm flat on the screen, he entered a ten-digit combination. With a hiss of escaping gas, the doors moved just a fraction. 'Can I get a hand?' he asked Big Ben. 'These are quite heavy.'

They were too, I could see, but once moving, they glided open, lights flickering on inside as the gap widened.

Standing closest, Big Ben got the first look inside, colourful expletives filling the air as he took in the view.

Curious, Jane, Amanda, my father, and I all rushed to see and found our own reason to swear. When Frank said he'd created somewhere to put his weapons, I'd failed to understand quite what he meant. In my head, he had a shotgun locker and a rack with a couple of swords. However, staring inside the room, I remembered the chest he lugged from under his table at the comic book stand in the castle when we faced the Klowns. From that came a double headed axe among other diabolical weapons including my own favourite, a baseball bat on which was written the legend 'Zombie Twatting Stick'.

Frank didn't own a few weapons. Frank owned an armoury.

'Oh. My. God,' muttered Amanda as her feet dragged her between the doors to explore inside.

The room had to be thirty feet deep and more than twenty feet across and it had racks fitted to every wall. There were more racks running down the middle so it was like walking into a library of weapons.

Big Ben asked, 'How are these arranged, Frank? By alphabet? Or by deadliness?' He was being flippant, but walking down one side of the room, I found myself overwhelmed by the scale of his collection.

'What are these for?' asked Jane, causing me to lean my head around the end of a rack to see what she had found.

'Those are stone axes with a copper core,' Frank explained as if that answered her question. Seeing her blank look, he added, 'For killing a hydra. The heads grow back if you don't use stone and they usually have several heads by the time they become a public nuisance so it's no good having one axe.'

'You didn't know that, Jane?' joked Big Ben, making it sound like it was general knowledge.

'Frank, these are guns,' said Amanda in her cop voice. 'This is highly illegal. You can't keep these.'

Frank tutted sadly. 'Until the police accept they can't defeat demons with a baton, or put a poltergeist in cuffs, every one of these weapons is necessary.'

'Do you have ammunition for them?' she asked, clearly hoping he would say no.

To her dismay, he opened a cabinet where hundreds of boxes in various calibres waited to be employed.

'Is this the bat you told me about, kiddo?' asked my dad, reaching up to take my twatting stick from the wall.

I chuckled to see it again. 'Yeah, that's the one.'

'You can forget that, Tempest,' said Frank. 'I have something much cooler for you to check out.' I looked across as he took a sword from a rack above his head. 'I was able to get a matched pair. I thought they might make a nice wedding present for Vermont Wensdale if he were ever to tie the knot, but until then …'

'It looks like a sword,' I observed, unsure why I should get excited about it. The twatting stick was just a bat; I only smiled at its memory because I'd used it on two occasions when it made the difference between living and dying.

With a flourish of his left hand as he held the sword in his right, Frank said, 'It's not just a sword. With a magic word it becomes something very much else – Incendius!' he ran his left hand up the sword's blade as it burst into flame.

Jane, standing closest, squealed, and jumped away. It shocked her enough that she forgot to use girl voice for a second and now looked embarrassed to have sounded like a man for a moment.

Big Ben moved closer, 'I have to hand it to you, Frank. That is something else. You said you have two?' He looked at the gap on the rack where the first one came from and selected its twin. Then he flourished it, looking like an oversized Peter Pan. 'Flame on!' he yelled.

'That's for the Human Torch,' I corrected him.

'The sword is enchanted, Big Ben,' sighed Frank. 'It requires the correct power word to make it work.' The flame went out on his sword. 'Here do it with me,' he offered, moving alongside my big friend to demonstrate. 'Say Incendius and run your hand up the blade, the flame will follow your fingers.'

Frank demonstrated, his sword bursting into flame once more. Big Ben looked sceptical but did it anyway, growling the magic word as he mimicked Frank's movements. Nothing happened.

I sniffed the air. 'Let me try,' I requested. Big Ben handed it over, pommel first, with a shrug. I lifted the pommel to inspect it, smiled to myself and cried, 'Incendius!' with passion. The flame leapt into life, illuminating the air around me.

Big Ben frowned. 'Magic?'

'There's a switch Frank failed to mention. It's a gas-powered sword. If you look closely,' I revealed, squinting through the flame at the blade, 'you can see tiny holes from which the gas is being ejected, and there's a charging hole in the side of the pommel which must double as a reservoir.'

Frank rolled his eyes. 'Okay, yes. They're props from a television program,' he admitted with a touch of irritation. His smile returned instantly though. 'They are seriously cool, though, aren't they? I got them for a song, only five grand each.'

I damned near dropped the one I held as I choked. Frank had way too much money to burn. The frivolity continued for a few more minutes but we were all tired, Frank included, and there was a mystery yet to solve.

Back upstairs, Jane insisted that she wasn't tired. Her body clock was a mess from staying up right through the previous night and then sleeping in past lunch. Pointing out that she was also the best person to dig around inside the McTavish's computer, we left her to crack on and went to bed.

Glimpsing the truth

I awoke the next morning partially intertwined with Amanda. I'd slept deeply which left me feeling both groggy and yet also refreshed. I needed to get up, get a shower, and drink some caffeine. If I ticked those boxes, I'd be ready for the day. However, when I attempted to slide myself away from the fragrant smelling mop of blonde hair on the pillow next to me, she awoke, and a hand snaked out to wrap around me.

A bout of wrestling ensued which delayed the start to my day in a most pleasing fashion. It then continued when she chose to follow me to the shower. Frank's folly needed a lot of work to update it, but the hot water worked and if he wanted a big creepy place to live in, he'd found it.

Downstairs, sipping tea and smiling at each other while some bread toasted, Amanda said, 'I didn't see Jane when I came through. She must have taken herself to bed at some point last night. Do you think she found anything?'

The toast popped, giving me a task to perform while I replied. 'She doesn't use a notepad to record notes like you

160

and I; she does everything on the computer, so I haven't been able to check. I thought about waking her, but I don't know where she went – there's so many rooms. It's early still; we should let her get a few hours sleep first. The computer is all hooked up. I think it's safe to assume she got it working and found her way around any passwords that might have been used.'

Amanda sipped her tea. 'I think she would have woken us if she'd found anything startling.' I passed Amanda a plate with two thick slices of wholemeal toast coated in a thicker layer of butter. 'What's next?' she asked.

'I'm leaving shortly to find Evan Allcorn. If I can,' I added. 'He doesn't answer the phone number Jane found for him and might not live at the address registered. I still haven't been able to speak to him or Mrs Moore about Dean Moore's Control Systems business. According to her, it was flourishing, but it no longer operates, and I want to know why. I also want to know why the loan sharks were after her, so next on my list after Evan Allcorn is to track them down. There's a big lie here somewhere.' I thought about that statement for a second. 'There's a big lie to do with Dean Moore. Then there's a huge secret to do with the Iraq war and Dean Moore's elite forces team. Monica Moore looks like she has plenty of money but if she is dead or bankrupt, we won't be getting paid.' Getting paid for this fiasco wasn't at the top of my priority list, surviving it was. Find out who the Undead are and stop them before they catch up to us and someone I love gets hurt – that was my priority.

'Evan Allcorn first then?' she checked.

I swallowed a bite of toast. 'Yes. I'm leaving in just a minute. Everyone else is asleep and they should stay that way for a while. I'll be back in a few hours to catch up with

Jane.' I pulled out my phone. 'I'm just going to send an email so Jane and Big Ben know where I am.'

She pushed back her chair, popping her last piece of toast into her mouth as she took her plate to the sink. 'I'm coming with you. I want to see your new toy.'

'Huh?' I paused in writing the email because I wasn't sure what she was saying.

'The car, Tempest. The gorgeous vintage Lotus you now seem to own. I need to hear the full story and I want to see it. Besides, I've barely seen you in the last few days with the werewolf case and now this one. I want to spend some time with you when we get to actually speak.'

That sounded good to me.

Outside, where we parked the cars, the snow was still falling. It wasn't coming down hard but there were two inches on top of the cars and the roads looked treacherous. 'It'll be fine when we reach the main roads,' I stated, not sounding at all sure we would make it that far.

'The Lotus is rear wheel drive?' she asked. When I nodded, she fished in her handbag for keys. 'Then we'd better take mine.' There would be opportunities to enjoy my new car later. I slid into her car and finished the email as she pulled away. I knew there were Apps I could get that would allow me to send text messages to multiple recipients, but my phone was already confusing enough. Emails I understood, so I let people know we were heading into Maidstone in Amanda's car and settled in for the ride.

The ride back to civilisation was a slow one, Amanda sensibly staying well below the speed limit as she forged through the snow, but as soon as we reached the A228 – the main road linking everything in the peninsula – we found it to be cleared and gritted.

My plan was to catch Evan Allcorn before he set off to

work. His LinkedIn profile showed him working for a small control systems firm which gave me a different place to try to find him if I struck out at his house. However, there were lights on at the address and every reason to believe he was home. The house was a pleasant looking detached home set back from the road. It wasn't an opulent property like Ramone Best occupied, but I would designate it as an upmarket family home.

A woman answered the door. 'Hello?' she said, peering out and wondering why there were two people on her doorstep at seven o'clock in the morning.

I let Amanda lead; her presence always seemed to calm people. 'Good morning,' she said with a big smile. 'We're terribly sorry to trouble you so early. Would it be possible to speak with Evan Allcorn?'

The woman's eyes twitched in surprise. A child's voice rang out behind her, wanting something done for them that appeared to be a task they couldn't perform for themselves. Over her shoulder, she called, 'Mummy won't be a minute, sweetie.' Then she turned back to face us. 'What is this about?'

'We're private investigators,' I explained. 'Mrs Moore, the wife of Dean Moore, Evan Allcorn's former business partner hired us. It really is imperative that I ask him some questions about the business.'

At the merest mention of the Moore's name, her face became a cloud of rage. I thought she was going to spit when she replied, 'That cow ruined my husband. Lied to him, took him to the cleaners, and stole all his money. I hope she rots in hell. Kindly tell her that when you next see her.'

'That's just the thing,' I kept my voice calm, 'she's gone missing. Is your husband home?'

She shook her head, still angry when she snapped, 'No. I kicked him out. He went to the bottle and became too unpredictable to have around the kids. He went to his mum's for a while, but I don't know where he is now. He hasn't called or texted me in a week.'

'Is he working?' Amanda asked.

Evan's wife just shrugged. 'Maybe. He got a job, but I don't know if he turns up for it or is too drunk.' Her shoulders sagged a little as her anger subsided. 'It really hit him hard, you know. He thought it was all going so well, but Dean had been fiddling the books. That's what Evan said. He told me Dean never paid any tax and had made all the money disappear. Evan didn't want to manage a firm, that's why he never set off by himself until he met Dean. Dean was all about managing the finances. What Evan didn't know was that Dean borrowed everything he could from the bank and when the bank wouldn't give him any more, he borrowed from people no sane person would borrow from. None of this came out until he died and by then it was too late. The bank came in and liquidated the firm's assets. Then, because Evan is a director, they had the right to come after his own money. The children's college funds, our cars, our savings. They took everything. If we owned the house, they would have taken that too. He filed for bankruptcy and started drinking.'

Amanda frowned. 'I missed something. You said Mrs Moore ripped him off.'

The angry mask returned. 'The day after Dean died in the car accident, she turned up here sobbing. She was a mess and of course we both gave her what comfort we could. She said she wanted to sell Dean's half of the business and claimed she couldn't bear to take over his business and be constantly reminded that he was gone. Evan bought her out. He borrowed a hundred thousand and bought her out. It was a dream come true he thought because suddenly, he would get all the profit from what he believed was a thriving company. The hundred thousand was a fraction of what the firm was worth and would be paid back in months. Three days later the bank turned up.'

I swallowed hard. If this was true, and I had no reason to disbelieve what I was hearing, then Mrs Moore was far from what I thought she was. I felt like I was glimpsing a truth for the first time, and it made me question everything I had seen until now.

As my eyes glazed over, I took a step back from the house. Amanda apologised once again for the intrusion, thanked Mrs Allcorn for her time and wished her well for the future. I heard her speaking but my brain was too busy racing to take any of it in.

Monica Moore had known her husband's business was a sham; that was the obvious conclusion and one I was ready to believe. He died after amassing massive debt which she then shook off onto an unsuspecting party while netting an additional six figure sum. Add that to the insurance pay out and the fact that he'd been making the profit, the loans, and the money owed to the taxman vanish into a black hole, I could draw yet another conclusion:

Dean Moore was still alive.

Monica Moore had lied about identifying the body. Just like Greta McTavish, she saw the body of another man lying in the morgue and claimed it to be her husband. Registered dead, she claimed the life insurance, then took all the money they had amassed and vanished.

Except she didn't vanish, she came to me and hired me to find out what was going on. It was making my head swim. I felt an arm loop through mine and turned to find

Amanda. Her lips were skewed to one side as if assessing me.

'You look like you're trying to divide pi by the square root of minus one,' she told me.

I shook my head as if trying to clear it. 'Why did she hire me?' I mumbled. 'I can't make sense of it.'

'You think Dean Moore is still alive, don't you?'

I nodded, my brain still whirling around inside my skull like someone had taken the top off and given it all a good stir. 'None of it makes sense. If she's in on it with Dean, then they planned the whole thing together. They scam the insurance firm, they steal the money from their own firm, and they rip off Dean's business partner. I don't know what that comes to, but it's over a million. Maybe well over. If she then vanishes with Dean, it makes sense. If she knows nothing about what is going on and Dean is genuinely dead, then she hires me because she thinks she is being followed. But if that's true, where is she now? Why did she rip off her husband's business partner? And best yet, is the daft Undead thing even related to her financial problems? I feel like I just caught sight of the truth, but it was fleeting and now it's gone again.'

'We should move on,' she suggested. 'Maybe we head to Maidstone police station and see how Quinn is getting on.' I went with her to the car where she opened my door and nudged me inside. I was operating on automatic while my brain dealt with higher functions like trying to work out what I had missed.

Maybe Quinn would have some answers.

The Paradox

'I have no answers.' Chief Inspector Quinn's reply made my head hurt just a little more. 'I think, Mr Michaels, that you and I are coming at this from two very different angles. I am investigating an incident where multiple assailants discharged firearms inside a gated community last night. You, in contrast, are chasing ghosts.'

The chief inspector made a regular habit of belittling my work and liked to suggest I was a ghost hunter even though he knew I was nothing of the sort. Drawing in a slow breath so I wouldn't rise to his goading, I said, 'They are not ghosts if they faked their deaths. I explained this last night.'

'You also assured me that Dean Moore was deceased, which he is. I checked the coroner's report. All the men you named are dead. You were right about the wives of the deceased as well. Three of them have missing person reports filed including Mrs Moore which I note has Miss Harper's name registered as the reporting person. There was no missing person report for Greta McTavish but if I

167

choose to believe that all six of the wives are now missing, I still don't have a crime to investigate.'

He could be a very frustrating man. I tried to make him see reason. 'I believe at least two of the men from that team are alive. Something happened in Iraq, and they have been hiding it for years while plotting to kill their team members and then vanish. If I am right, the two left alive are the last two to die. That's no coincidence. They killed their former colleagues, killed their wives, then faked their own deaths and disappeared with the money. I think they took the money their former colleagues had, but they have been watching to see if anyone would sniff at their trail.'

The chief inspector frowned deeply. 'Didn't you just finish telling me that Mrs Moore must have falsely identified her husband's body? Why then did she hire you and report that she thought her husband was back from the dead?' He had me there. I didn't want him to see that I felt defeated by the confusion of this case, but he was alert and intuitive enough to know when he had the upper hand. 'I see,' he said of my silence.

'Did you get anywhere with the phone?' I asked. 'They have been contacting me but haven't bothered to shield their number.'

He shook his head in a disappointed way. 'It's a cheap burner phone that can be bought in any supermarket. There's no requirement to register them.'

I sat forward in my chair and gave him an open and honest expression. 'I have stumbled across something, and I don't know what it is. An entire special forces team are listed as dead, and their wives are all missing. I took Mrs Moore's case and since then I have been threatened, had to move twice, had my parents' house invaded, had my friend's house mostly destroyed and all within a forty-eight-hour period. One or more of that team are still alive and their attacks and threats are all because they fear I will uncover the truth.'

'What truth?'

I sat back in the chair again. 'That's the question I'm working on, but I think it has more than one answer. There's a truth behind what happened in Iraq to cause all this but that's not what they care about, they are worried I will prove they are alive. Leave the dead to be dead, that was the warning they first sent me. They called themselves Undead Incorporated.' The chief inspector knew this already.

Ian Quinn held his hands in front of his face and steepled his fingers. 'Let's say our enquiries are one and the same.' I wanted to rage that they were, and that it was patently obvious, but I held my tongue. 'I am willing to work with you for the sake of public safety. What do you propose as your next move?'

'I was going to track down the loan shark I had a fight with in Swanley, but I see no sense in that now. Your computer forensic team need to turn their attention to finding Mrs Moore. If she has been taken against her will, then she may already be dead. That's assuming I am wrong about Dean Moore being alive and her being complicit in the faking of his death. If I am right, then she is with them and possibly our best chance of finding them, is in finding her, but whatever facial recognition software you have, it needs to be attuned to find Dean and Monica Moore, Rob McTavish and possibly his wife too.'

He blew a hard breath out through his nose. 'Mrs Moore coming to you makes no sense whatsoever,' Quinn argued. 'The only reason there is any investigation is because she came to you. If she is complicit, mentioning it to anyone is the dumbest thing she can possibly do. If she isn't guilty, then she wouldn't have falsely identified her husband's body, in which case he really is dead, and you would yet again have me chasing ghosts.'

I wanted to beat my head against a wall. He was right. I knew it and he knew it. The paradox I faced was that Mrs Moore had to be involved yet also couldn't be. No matter which way I twisted the story in my head, I just couldn't get it to fit.

When I got back to the reception area, escorted by a young female officer, Amanda pushed away from the front desk and waved goodbye to whoever she'd been chatting with. 'How'd it go?' she asked. Her relationship with her former boss was such that she would quite happily watch him drown for a while before reluctantly throwing him a life buoy, so it was no surprise to me when she insisted on waiting in reception while I wasted my time talking to him.

Grumpily, I said, 'We're on our own.'

The snow had stopped, but the icy chill hit us the moment the automatic doors swished open. It rarely gets below freezing in our neck of the woods, and the temperature was a shock. If I'd been at home, I would be fishing out my ski jacket and walking boots. Living out of a bag as we stayed away from places the Undead might expect to spot us, I had to manage with a pair of leather oxfords and a designer coat.

The car park at the station is often full. So often, in fact, that we didn't even bother to check it. Amanda's car was across the street in a public car park. Waiting for traffic to pass so we could cross the road, I told her, 'He reinforced his desire to put us all in protective custody. I shouldn't have told him we are the target, now he thinks he can defuse the situation by hiding us somewhere.' I was being grumpy about it because he refused to understand hiding us would do nothing but mask the problem, not deal with it. Feeling off kilter because I couldn't figure out Mrs Moore, I continued, quite uncharacteristically, to moan all the way back to her car.

Keeping quiet as I whined about my malfunctioning brain and about Chief Inspector Quinn's inability to help, Amanda took out her keys and pointed the fob at her car. It beeped once, then blinding white light flash-fried my retinas as the Mini Cooper exploded in a blinding ball of fire.

On the Run

I knew I'd lost consciousness because there was no sense of passing time and when I opened my eyes there were people all around me and I wasn't where I had been. Deep panic drove me upwards from my prone position. 'Amanda!'

'Here, Tempest! I'm here,' she called to me, coughing deeply. I could see her spitting blood into the snow as I turned my head to find her.

Ten yards away, the Mini was a swirling ball of orange flames and thick black smoke. Police officers were with us, and now I was sitting up, I could see where they must have grabbed our hands or arms to drag us away from the inferno. It could be no more than a minute or so since the explosion as, glancing around, the police were still trying to deal with traffic in the street running alongside the carpark as drivers gawped from their windows. The fire brigade was yet to arrive; another indication of how little time had elapsed.

'Are you alright?' I shouted over the ringing in my ears. Amanda wasn't missing any body parts. In fact, apart from a trace of blood on her lips from coughing it up, the only mark on her was a thin trickle of blood coming down from her hair line.

We had been incredibly lucky. She plipped the car open when we were still more than five yards away. Had we been closer, it might have killed us both or inflicted terrible, life-changing wounds. It didn't bear thinking about.

'Stay still, sir,' advised an officer kneeling by my side. 'Paramedics are on their way.'

Pain reports were coming in from various parts of my body: my back, my shoulders, my skull. I felt the back of my head and found blood on my fingertips when I looked at them. Ignoring the officer's wise advice, I levered myself off the ground. If the Undead were watching, I wanted them to know I was still functioning. I was mad now – not that I wasn't before – but I was fed up fighting blind. I was in a boxing ring with a blindfold on and my opponent kept punching me. Even though I could fight back, I couldn't see them.

Amanda held her hand out for me to help her up too. 'It's too cold to be lying on the ground,' she told the nearest police officers as they opened their mouths. Staring at the flames, she said, 'I liked that car.'

I put my arm around her. 'We'll get you another one.'

'It had my favourite lipstick in it.'

'We'll get another one of those too.'

'And my *Frozen* singalong CD,' she complained.

I couldn't stop myself from laughing, which had been her intention. We both laughed and I hoped the Undead were watching as we guffawed and the police officers exchanged questioning looks and wondered what had gotten into us.

Movement to my right made me look that way. The officers were moving aside to let Chief Inspector Quinn through. 'Are you both okay?' he asked, dealing with the formality of checking our health first. When we assured him we were fine, he pursed his lips and nodded. 'I'm afraid it is now necessary to insist upon protective custody. For public safety reasons, I am able to …'

Amanda cut him off. 'I know the law, Ian. And I know how you are choosing to use it to get what you want.'

'We'd love to,' I cut in. I got a surprised look from Quinn and a horrified look from Amanda.

'Tempest, we can't,' she protested.

'It's the only sensible option now, babe,' I squeezed her hand. I didn't mean a word of it but had no way of expressing that with so many people within earshot. Going into protective custody would get us nothing unless Quinn and his team were able to solve the case and find the Undead. I had not one jot of faith that he would even look in the right direction. Finding dead people was my thing, not his.

A wink at Amanda would get the message across but I daren't try that either because there were too many people who might see, Quinn included, so I held her hand and waited. An opportunity to express my true intentions would arise soon – arranging protective custody wasn't something that could happen by clicking one's fingers.

Waiting for that opportunity took longer than expected.

Escorted back inside the station to wait for the paramedics, we were at least able to warm up. I also used my phone to call Big Ben.

'Hey, short round,' he hallooed into the phone. 'How did you and Blondie get on this morning?'

'We're at Maidstone police station. We're going to need a lift.'

'Something happened to her car?'

'It exploded.'

I got a beat of silence in response before he said. 'We are fast running out of cars.'

I couldn't argue with that. 'Good point. I'll hire one. Something that can deal with the snow.' There was a rental place near the rail station about half a mile away. Paramedics in their green uniform arrived at a run with two officers escorting them. We were in the depths of the station, hanging out in a lounge/meal area with tables, chairs, and a big screen television. 'We're just getting checked out. We'll be back soon.' I let him know.

'You're okay?' he wanted to know.

'Bruises. Nothing more. These guys are starting to annoy me though,' I replied in a deliberately understated way. 'Is Jane up?'

'Not yet.'

I sucked on my teeth. 'Okay. Gotta go. Give me an hour. We should be back by then.'

The paramedics arrived and it occurred to me we could just go with them to the hospital and slip away from protective custody from there, but I felt certain Quinn would send someone to guard and keep an eye on us. There was no reason to go to hospital, so we answered their questions, let them give us a quick check over and dismissed them. That still took forty minutes as they wanted to be thorough.

When they left, we both excused ourselves to visit the restrooms. We weren't exactly being watched; CI Quinn appointed an officer to be with us while someone else, a team for all I knew, went through the process of organising somewhere for the police to squirrel us away. However, the officer supposedly watching us, clearly thought he didn't need to be all that vigilant – we were inside a police station -

and was too busy watching a show on the television to pay us any attention. Probably happy to have been given an easy, indoor task where he could relax and stay warm, he was going to catch hell from Quinn when he discovered we were gone. I couldn't manage to feel bad about that.

Amanda took my hand and led me through the station to a door at the rear. No one gave us a second glance as we stole away into the cold again. We were on the run from the police in a way, while also fleeing an unseen enemy.

I can admit that my nerves were jangling as I looked about for anyone who might be looking our way. Mercifully, no one jumped out to prove my paranoia justified as we left the police station behind us. Across the street a fire crew were still dealing with the partly molten wreckage of Amanda's car, and there were police with them which made us hold our breath when we passed close on our way to the city centre.

We hurried on, turning up our collars against the chill wind. The pavements were covered in slushy snow; slippery underfoot as it melted, but not so dangerous that people were falling over. As we neared the car rental office by the train station at the other end of the High Street, a shadow moved inside, and I tensed.

Until Big Ben stepped out through their door. He waved a hello and said, 'I figured I could rent a car or two and come find you.'

'How did you get here?' asked Amanda just before Frank popped his head around the door.

'Hi, guys,' he said, a big smile on his face.

Big Ben held the door open to let Frank out, then stepped out himself to be followed by a chap wearing a coat with the rental firm's logo. He carried a clipboard and had keys in his hand.

Big Ben said, 'Jane messaged. She's found something. We need to get back to Frank's.'

Ten minutes later, we were all on the road. Frank left his car with the rental chaps – they had a car park with spaces – so he was in one Land Rover with Big Ben, and Amanda was with me in another. They were perfect for the conditions, but expensive to replace. In light of our current situation, Big Ben had taken out everything insurance.

I drove at Amanda's request, doing my best to be watchful for anything that might indicate trouble, and for the traffic which was a struggle because my brain was still busily trying to unravel the ball of knots it had become.

Through the Medway Towns and over the river, we drove onward back to Frank's house. I felt I couldn't relax, poised on the edge of my seat as I waited for machine gun fire to target the cars. Even when we left the towns behind and had clear fields all around us, I still feared for a sniper out of sight on a hill half a mile away. Only when we were back at Frank's house, did I finally feel I could slow my heart rate.

Jane was waiting for us and literally bouncing with excitement. 'Come on, guys,' she insisted. 'You have to see this.' Then she paused and looked at Amanda, whose hair and makeup were a mess still, and then at me. I looked like I'd fallen into a pile of slushy snow … because I had. 'What happened to you two?' she asked.

'I guess Big Ben didn't tell you,' I replied. 'It's nothing but a distraction. What did you find?'

'It's on the computer you took from Robert McTavish. The document folders were all deleted and the recycle bin had been emptied.'

Frank raised his hand to get her attention. 'Doesn't that mean they are gone for good?'

She gave him a patient smile. 'There is a common misconception that files are completely removed from computer hard drives when we delete them. The fact is that any time a file is deleted on a hard drive, it's not erased. Instead, only the tiny bit of information that points to the location of the file on the hard drive is erased. This pointer, along with other pointers for every folder and file on the hard drive, is saved in a section near the beginning of the hard drive and is used by the operating system to compile the directory tree structure. By erasing the pointer file, the actual file becomes invisible to the operating system. And that means you can write new data over the area where the old file is located. However, if you haven't written new information over it, the file is still there. I used a simple file recovery program to reinstall the whole drive. Then I had to painstakingly go through each file to see if anything was worth looking at.'

'And you found something,' I prompted, hoping she would get to the point.

With a grin she told us, 'I found a folder with saved emails. It was probably long forgotten since it was dated January 15th almost two years ago, but it gave me two email addresses. One for the recipient, Robert McTavish, and one for the sender. The sender's email address is dangermouse101@blueyonder.co.uk which could be anyone if the sender hadn't signed it Vince at the bottom.'

'You're saying we have a message between Vince and Rob.' I still wanted her to get to the point. 'What did it say?'

'Nothing of interest. They were talking about fishing off the coast of Malta. It sounded as if they had something planned but the email I found didn't go into any detail about it. I think it got saved because it had an attached picture.' She stopped talking and locked eyes with me. I was becoming frustrated but keeping it in check. 'Don't you see?' she asked. 'The email was dated almost two years ago.' She continued to stare at me.

Amanda got it first. 'Vince had been dead for a year by then.'

It was the lightning bolt moment again when all my electrons fired at once. Was I tired? Was that why I couldn't see the point Jane had been making? Vince sent an email a year after his death. Getting a grip of myself, I said, 'It doesn't prove Vince sent it. Only that it was signed off with his name. It could be someone else called Vince. It might be a total red herring.'

'But you don't believe that,' stated Big Ben.

I hung my head. 'No, I don't.' Then more electricity fried my nerves. 'The photographs!' I didn't stop to explain, I simply turned and bolted, running back toward Frank's front door. With all that happened last night and the lateness of the hour, I'd left the pile of paperwork Big Ben took from Rob McTavish's house in the car. I was going back for it last night but never got there.

I slipped on the snow, righted myself, and fumbled for the keys. A minute after running from the room, I was back with everyone and looking for a space on the table where I could spread out the contents of my arms.

'We're looking for pictures of a reunion that took place two years ago. Rob's sister said they all got together down at the beach. Spread the paperwork out and shout if you find any pictures. We all got to it, sifting and moving the paperwork into piles. Big Ben explained that he found a file drawer in the desk the computer sat on. I didn't give him a chance to look through it at the time, but his cursory inspection revealed photographs of something, so he'd scooped everything in the entire draw.

Within seconds, my mother shouted that she'd found something. For once it wasn't a bottle of wine. Holding a picture aloft in her right hand and a white envelope in her left, I could see a casual unposed shot of some chaps drinking beer from cans and chatting while a barbeque smoked on the ground by their feet. It wasn't just guys though, there were women with them.

I had to race around the table to see it, Big Ben getting there first. 'That's Martin Kemp,' he said, taking the photograph from my mother's hand and placing it on the table. More pictures spilled out and the evidence was damning. 'And that's Greta McTavish.'

Looking over his shoulder, I pointed to a blonde woman. 'That's Monica Moore. I guess she dyed her hair back then.' We could see them all: Beefy, Vince Barnes, Andrew 'Martin' Kemp, Dean, Rob, and Edgar 'Ginge' Salter. All six were there but if the picture was less than two years old, at least two of them were dead when it was taken. Add to that the two I already believed were alive and the picture of what we faced became much clearer.

'That's Vince's wife, Shania,' Big Ben pointed out a petite woman caught mid-laugh.

'How do you know?' I asked. I couldn't have named any of the wives and only knew Monica because I'd met her this week, and Greta because I'd recently seen her picture at her parents' place. Big Ben gave me a look that let me know I was being dumb: he'd slept with her. Of course he had.

I pulled out my phone, flicked through the numbers I had and realised I hadn't taken one for Rob's sister, Alice Cumber. 'Jane, I need a number for Alice Cumber in Barry. She's Rob's sister.'

Jane pulled an oops face. 'My laptop is defragmenting.

I've been running it hard the last few days. For optimal performance ...'

I waved for her to stop. 'Just use mine,' I said with a smile. 'It's right there.'

'What's your password?' she asked, flipping it open.

'Ooh, I bet it's something really cheesy or stupid,' laughed Big Ben. 'Is it something to do with Amanda and her interest in small men with small p ...' Amanda slapped the back of his head which stopped him completing his sentence.

I leaned over Jane to enter the password myself and two minutes later, I was listening to Alice Cumber's phone ring and praying she would pick up. When she did, I barely let her get a word in before I blurted my response. 'Alice, it's Tempest Michaels. We found the pictures of the reunion. When exactly did you say it was?'

'Oh, um, I'm not rightly sure,' she replied, stumbling to answer my question now she was on the spot.

I pressed her to give me something I could work with. 'A month would be close enough. What month was it? What season?'

'Och, it was summer. June. No, hold on. I remember now. It was July. That Andy Murray was playing at Wimbledon. It was the middle Saturday, and he had a third-round match. I remember being upset that I couldnae watch it because Rob was getting together with all his old army buddies and I'd promised to go along.'

There it was. A date reference that put two dead men firmly in the frame for being still alive. They'd be using fake names and probably had fake passports. I thought it likely they didn't even live in the country.

'Thank you, Alice.'

'Is that all, love?' she sounded disappointed, and I

remembered she expected a message from her missing brother. She still thought he was coming to rescue her from her dismal life.

I wasn't sure what to say, and I didn't want to lie. So I said, 'For now, Alice. That's all for now.'

When I ended the call, all eyes around the table were facing my way.

'They're all alive, aren't they,' said Big Ben. I didn't need to answer, we all believed it was true. 'We are up against a squad of former Special Ops Squadron soldiers who have access to weapons and explosives and are officially dead,' he summed up.

'What do we do, Tempest?' asked my mother. She looked rightfully worried.

My phone rang before I could answer her, and it was no surprise to see CI Quinn's name displayed as the caller. 'Where are you, Mr Michaels?' he asked without bothering to say hello. 'I have cars at your home, your office, and at the addresses of all your known associates.' He hadn't thought to check up on Frank.

'They are all alive,' I told him. 'The entire team. We have just uncovered evidence that shows two of them attending an event after they were buried.'

'More ghost stories, Mr Michaels?' he sighed.

'You want to catch the people that shot up a building last night and blew up a car in a public car park today? You already have their names. Get their faces on TV and give them nowhere to hide, Chief Inspector.

'You have evidence?' he sounded interested at least.

'Photographs which were taken after two of the men were killed. Their missing wives are there too.' I felt like I was repeating myself.

He poked a hole in my claim. 'Is there a date on the photograph, something to show when it was taken?'

My shoulders sagged, and around the table my friends and family threw their hands in the air. 'No. Not a damned thing,' I growled angrily. 'Choose to believe me or don't. How many times have I solved big cases now when it could have been you? Are you going to let another one slip through your fingers?'

A few months ago, he would have hung up the phone on me, or spat a retort, but since then, he'd learned to pay attention when I said I knew what was going on. 'Let's say I choose to believe you, Mr Michaels. I cannot go on television claiming to know who the terrorist group are without absolute proof. That's just not how it's done. The chief constable would demote me on the spot. And what if you are wrong? I am the one who will look the fool. The men you claim to be behind this are dead. That is what I can prove. An undated photograph backed by an ironclad Tempest Michaels hunch, isn't going to change the public course of my investigation.'

'And what the public cannot see?' I pushed him.

He huffed a heavy breath. 'I will, of course, divert resources to check your claims when you submit yourself for protective custody.'

His caveat made me snap. 'If we hadn't left the station, we wouldn't have been able to prove they are all alive!' I raged.

'You haven't proven it!' he shouted back.

'I have a photograph of them taken after they died!' I think this was the first time we had actually shouted at each other.

'That's not proof!' he yelled.

Forcing myself to be calm, I unclenched my jaw. 'Ian, I

am going to scan and send you the pictures and provide you with a contact for the sister of Rob McTavish. She attended the event and will testify to the date it took place and who was in attendance. In the meantime, since you refuse to play ball, I am going to find the men in question and kill them.'

A moment of stunned silence followed, both at his end and at mine as my friends and family all stared at me. They all had open mouths except Big Ben, who was grinning. CI Quinn cleared his throat. 'Mr Michaels, you just informed a senior police officer of your intention to murder six men. I can have you arrested.'

'No, actually you cannot,' I argued, amusement giving an edge to my words.

'Explain,' he replied in a bored tone.

'You don't know where I am for a start, Ian. However, the more important element is that the men I propose to kill are already dead. Isn't that the lie you are hiding behind?' I heard him draw a breath to argue and cut him off, 'Good day, Chief Inspector.'

A jab of the red button ended the call. I didn't know if he might try to call back, but he wouldn't get any joy if he did. A deep breath helped to still my nerves, which were jangling and hopped up on adrenalin from the verbal battle.

'Do you want me to send him the picture still?' asked Jane, breaking the silence.

I nodded. 'Yes. We have a duty to help the police even if they are pig-headed and ignorant.'

With a quiet voice, my mother asked, 'Do you really plan to kill them, Tempest?'

Looking around the room, it seemed everyone wanted to hear my answer to that question. 'No, mum,' I replied, my voice as quiet as hers had been. 'Not if I can avoid it. I don't want to fight them, let alone kill them, or anyone for that matter, but I'm not sure they are going to give me a choice.'

'They won't stop, Tempest,' said Big Ben. 'It's not in their nature, and we can't keep letting them attack us. We have to find a way to take the fight to them.'

From across the room, Jane said, 'Um, guys.' Big Ben, who had his back to her, turned around and we all looked across to where she was sitting at my laptop. 'I think I know how they have been keeping tabs on us.' Seeing she had our attention she explained. 'I'm not the only one using your laptop.'

I moved toward her. 'What are you saying?'

She swivelled in her chair, pointing to a corner of the screen. 'There's a spy inside your laptop.'

'A spy?' repeated my mother. 'What does that mean?'

'Malicious software,' Frank explained, which didn't help my mother to understand what was being discussed.

Jane was delving into the background workings and directory systems of the computer as we gathered around her. 'Frank's right,' she said. 'These things are sophisticated and hard to detect. I only spotted it because I noticed your email outbox folder had an outgoing email just after I sent the email to the chief inspector. Whatever else this is doing, it's generating additional emails each time one is sent. It's probably also copied your entire directory and linked itself to your phone and other devices. Once it's inside, it can get everywhere.'

'They've been onto us from the start,' whispered Amanda.

Dad asked, 'How did it get in there?'

'Probably attached to an email,' said Jane. 'Tempest's email and phone number are on the website and displayed on advertisements. An email arrives on his computer and he wouldn't even have to open it; all it would take is a click to send it to his deleted items folder and the spyware would start to work.'

'Stupid computers,' growled my mother. 'Ungodly things. I always said no good would come from them. I watched that *Terminator* film. They'll take over the world and kill us all.'

Ignoring her, dad asked, 'You can remove it, right? Shut them down and cut off their access?'

Jane said, 'Sure. It'll take a while, but I have some software to seek and destroy this thing once I identify it.' Her fingers started to dance across the keyboard.

I put a hand on her shoulder. 'Don't.' My request made everyone look at me with a question on their lips.

All except Big Ben, who said, 'Bait the hook and reel them in?'

Baiting the Hook

'You're not going to lure them here, are you?' asked Frank cagily. He had a house in a remote location with secret passages, plus a dungeon, and thick walls. It was an ideal location to bring them to. But it also probably wasn't.

'If they come here, they will stand outside and shoot grenades through every window before setting fire to it. They won't storm it unless they have to, which they won't. The house would become a death trap for us. Besides, I want them to feel they have the upper hand.'

Big Ben tapped the laptop to get our eyes on it. 'Right now, they are looking at the email Jane sent with the picture of them all at the reunion last year. They will see that we sent it to Chief Inspector Quinn, so they most likely think the cat is out of the bag. They will want to run.'

'But they are arrogant,' I added. 'They won't run quickly. They won't believe they can be caught, so they will be taking their time, and they might even tell themselves that one photograph isn't enough. I think we send Quinn another email in which we point out that the picture doesn't have a date on it.'

'I can do that,' said Jane.

'Then what?' Frank wanted to know.

There was a plan slowly forming in my head. I wanted to run away from it, but I didn't see how I could. 'Then we show them something they will not be able to resist. We exhume Dean Moore's body.'

Jane said, 'Ewwww,' and my mother crossed herself.

'We're not actually going to dig his body up,' I reassured them. 'I have no desire to see inside his coffin. Of course, once this is done, I expect the police will dig up all the coffins. There are six dead men in them who are not the person listed on the headstone.'

'What about the wives?' asked Amanda. 'Do you think they are here with the men?'

I didn't. 'I'm still confused about Monica Moore's role. Dean Moore is still alive which means she falsely identified his body, or she identified it but couldn't tell it wasn't him.'

'I guess that's possible,' said my father, not sounding at all convinced that it was.

'Improbable though,' I reasoned. 'Mrs Moore was specific in her details. He had a tattoo that she used to identify his body and it was aged. That's not something you can fake.'

'Yes, it is,' argued Jane, looking up from the laptop screen. 'It's becoming quite popular. You mentioned it two days ago and I should have said something then. Its relevance didn't occur to me at the time. Sorry.'

Big Ben's face matched mine. 'Pre-aged tattoos?' he asked.

'It's relatively new,' she said, then because we were

giving her disbelieving looks, she opened a search bar and found a local tattoo artist whose website offered them.

Shaking my head ruefully, I said, 'They killed a person of similar size, put a tattoo on him and made sure his face was destroyed in the crash.' Mother crossed herself again. 'That takes care of the identification part of it. Even if the coroner suspected something, or found an anomaly, they would never question the tattoo. But why did she then come to me?'

'Cold feet?' asked Amanda.

'Maybe the wives are dead, and she finally caught on?' suggested Big Ben.

'We know the wives are alive,' Jane reminded him.

'Oh yeah,' he remembered. 'Maybe she didn't want to go on the run with Dean,' he tried a different theory. 'Maybe she was fed up with him. She gets the money, or rather, she had the money because he is pretending to be dead while she is still alive, but she decides to keep it for herself.'

I paused what I was thinking to look at him. 'You might be onto something there.'

'Then where is she?' asked Amanda.

'Where are any of them?' I replied. 'I think it's time we found out.'

Amanda came in close to me, putting her hand on my arm. 'Tempest, are you really going to go up against this team? We don't even know how many there are.'

She was right to be concerned but while her fear was increasing, I was beginning to feel calmer. Now that I believed I knew what I was up against, a plan was forming. I gave her hand a pat. 'I need to send an email,' I announced to the room.

Jane left the chair in front of my laptop, sliding out of

the way so I could get in. 'Are you sending it to them?' asked my father.

'To Big Ben,' I explained. 'They'll see it anyway, right, Jane?'

Jane said, 'The emails are going somewhere. My assumption is that the spyware is theirs. Sending them a baited message is one way to find out. Once you're done there, if I can have your laptop for a while, I think I can find exactly where the emails are going.'

Tapping out my email to Big Ben, I said, 'Super.'

Confused by what was happening, my mother asked, 'Why are you emailing Big Ben when he is stood three feet away?'

'This is the lure, mum. They have known where we were going to be because they were picking up my messages. They knew we went to Scotland and that they could attack Big Ben's place, and that Amanda and I went to Maidstone in her car this morning. They have always been one step or more ahead of us. Now it's our turn. I can predict that they are going to be in a graveyard in a few hours because they will be there to stop Big Ben and me from digging up Dean Moore's body.' I finished the email asking Big Ben to meet me at the cemetery to enact our plan and clicked the send button.

'What then?' asked my mother.

Drone Work

It felt strange to have the pace of our investigation slow for once. Instead of racing forward to the next task, we stopped. There was work to do, and research we could perform but with the lure in place, we couldn't spring the trap until it was late evening. So we watched a movie.

That wasn't all we did, obviously. But we honest to goodness all stopped for a couple of hours and watched a film on Frank's television. Dad cuddled on one couch with mum, Amanda snuggled into me, and we let the pace of life ease while we drank tea and ate cookies.

Of course, by the time we sat down to watch the film, Big Ben and I had snuck back to the Blue Moon office in Rochester to collect my drones, one of which we then had to repair because some of the rotor blades were damaged a few days ago. We fixed it and performed a test run. We also ransacked Frank's dungeon for weapons. Amanda did not approve and I could see her point of view: running around England with loaded guns would land me in jail, but it was

191

one thing to go up against these guys, and another entirely to do it unarmed. Selecting small calibre handguns, we cleaned, oiled, loaded and test fired them in the woods. Reassured they would work if we needed them to, we all settled in to relax on the couches.

Believing Dean and his cohort would read the email and decide they needed to act, we figured they would be at the graveyard early. In the email, I'd suggested a meeting time of 2100hrs and made it look like we were coming from different locations. They would get there long before our expected arrival time to search the area, make themselves familiar with it, and plan where to catch and kill us.

That was why we got there four hours before them and watched them arrive.

Horsten cemetery, where Dean Moore's body was laid to rest, was not far from their house in Swanley. Located in an older part of the town, it was nestled between houses on one side and a school on the other. At the leading edge was a road and at the rear it faded onto woodland which ran to the M25 motorway a few hundred yards beyond. There were obvious entry points where gates were located, but the Undead wouldn't use them. They wouldn't arrive in cars and park in the street either; they would sneak in through the woods at the back.

Having learned from them all those years ago, we knew to get there and perform our own search of the area, picking obvious routes in and out. They could park their cars half a mile away and approach through the trees. The ground sloped down to the road which meant they would also have the high ground.

They moved through the woods in two teams of three with slow, deliberate movements, sneaking up on the target and then fanning out so they could cross the open ground.

Using our drones, Big Ben and I watched the whole thing from the flat roof of a classroom, having broken into the school grounds. Our cars were likewise half a mile away, but we'd parked ours up the street at the front of the graveyard, knowing they would expect us to approach that way later.

Employing the thermal cameras fitted to the drones, the six man team – I cannot tell you how relieved I was that there were only six of them and not a whole platoon – were easy to spot and track as they patrolled the cemetery, pinpointed Dean Moore's grave, and moved away back into the woods.

The next bit was trickier because it involved putting ourselves in harm's way. I tried to convince Amanda, Frank, and my dad to stay behind at Frank's house, but they point blank refused to hear of it. Mum raged at dad and stormed off when he told her to pipe down, and Jane was working on my laptop, doing something, she told me, though she failed to elaborate on what it was.

There were five of us at the graveyard, all hidden from sight and praying the Undead weren't also using drones with thermal cameras because if they were, our attempt at hiding would be quite pointless.

'You're sure you want to do this?' asked Amanda.

I nodded, forcing my face to look more confident than I felt. 'It's the right move. We need them to decide to run now. I want them nervous enough to go to where they go when they feel a need to regroup.' I kissed her and started moving away. 'I'll be back in a few minutes.'

We went back for the cars, jogging along the tree-lined avenue beneath the streetlights in our black combat gear. If anyone saw us, they would likely call the cops, but it was late enough and the location remote enough, that no cars passed us, and we met no one out walking their dog.

The Undead would be watching down the gentle slope for us to arrive. They expected two men with shovels so that was what we were going to show them. We wore radios fitted over our left ears to give us secure communications between our small group. Necessary for what we were going to now do.

Parking in front of the graveyard gates, we made sure we were visible when the interior lights came on. 'They are moving,' dad's voice echoed in my ear.

'One group or both?' asked Big Ben.

'Just one,' he clarified.

It was what we expected. One would remain in place to give covering fire, the other would move forward to kill us. Covering fire was completely unnecessary, but their training was firmly entrenched it seemed.

In the cemetery, the light from the street faded away. The moon was hidden behind the clouds but the snow on the ground, and on every other surface, reflected the small amount of light there was. It worked against us as it made us highly visible. The Undead approaching us had the trees behind them so they were invisible to us for now.

'How far out from the trees are they?' I asked. Amanda and Frank were controlling the drones now, tucked away and out of sight, but my father, just a few feet from them, had a fun surprise in store for our unsuspecting dead people.

'About ten yards,' replied Amanda.

'Now?' asked Dad.

Big Ben and I both took our handguns from their pouches and raised them ready. 'On a count of three, dad. Three, two, one.' I said the words quietly despite the adrenalin pumping through my veins and as I said, 'one,' Big Ben and I split and ducked.

To the Undead approaching us from the trees, it would have looked like we vanished from sight as we hid behind two gravestones we'd picked out earlier. I believed it would sow a seed of confusion and doubt, but the whump of something to our right would definitely give them pause.

Among Frank's fun collection of weapons and stuff were a box of hand-held illumination rounds. Much like a firework, the user needed only to point the business end at the sky and pull the pin. Dad fired three of them, sending balls of burning phosphorus into the night sky. Reaching a height of three hundred feet, they would then slowly return to Earth under a small parachute while doing a spectacular job of bathing the graveyard in fake sunlight.

Instantly visible, three of the Undead team were caught in the open.

Big Ben poked his head out. 'That's jolly sporting of them,' he joked as he lined up his arm and squeezed the trigger.

Despite my statement to the Chief Inspector about being able to kill them without fear of prosecution, I knew it wasn't true. I fired two aimed rounds of my own but neither of us were aiming to kill. We were aiming for their legs, but we missed, much as expected. Most handguns, unlike they often show on the movies, have an effective range of less than one hundred yards. Much beyond that and the bullet has lost so much velocity that it might bounce off the target instead of go through it. They are not accurate either, despite what Hollywood might have us believe.

The Undead were stunned to have been ambushed, the three caught in the open momentarily motionless until they heard us shoot at them. Then they burst for cover, finding gravestones of their own to hide behind.

I heard it when one shouted for cover fire, demanding

the static team at the edge of the woods start shooting to pin us down so they could withdraw.

Into my radio, I whispered, 'Do it now, Dad.'

From his protected position on the roof of the school way over to the right of the graveyard, my father took aim at the general area the drone screen showed him the second team were in. He had a longbow to which an arrow with an exploding tip was fitted. Frank had the most glorious collection of weapons. Which was fun provided we didn't get caught using them.

The blind shot sailed high into the air; not that I could see it, but I knew it would be coming down any second. Just as the second team opened fire, the arrow hit the upper branches of a tree and exploded.

'Ha, ha! Boom!' yelled my father, his voice carrying over the radio clearly.

There was no fireball, yet again that's a Hollywood thing: Grenades don't create fireballs and neither do small exploding arrowheads because there's nothing inside them to burn. They do send out shrapnel though along with a wave of kinetic energy that will sweep along anything loose or not completely stuck down.

In this case, it blasted out bits of tree and shrapnel and made the snow in the trees dump to the floor in one go. I couldn't tell how close Dad had got with his shot, but a cry of pain told me someone was hurt.

Confusion reigned as the Undead suffered a moment of disorientation – they hadn't expected to be attacked or for us to use weapons against them. However, these were some of the best trained soldiers in the world and they weren't given to panic.

Someone shouted an order, 'Wait for the illumination to fall!'

'No time!' someone else shouted in response. 'The police will be coming!' The illumination rounds were drifting closer to the ground, casting long shadows, and making it easier to hide. Both Big Ben and I had belly crawled from where we were to new positions. I suspected they would have too, but the voice gave me a direction to look and when he broke cover to run for the trees, I popped up to loose a pair of rounds in his direction.

Incredibly, I hit him, his yell letting me know at least one of the rounds had found some flesh. My moment of celebration had to be short-lived as my own movement had given the team in the trees something to aim at.

The headstone to my front exploded as high-calibre rounds chewed it up. Injured or not, they were able to provide cover now, but we had given them reason to question how many they were up against and they were going to retreat.

Glancing quickly, I could see three figures running between the headstones to get back to the woods. One was moving more slowly than the others; the one I'd hit no doubt. But they were going to escape and that was perfect.

Into my microphone, I said, 'Time to pack it up, team. Let's get out of here before the police arrive.' Then, because I knew my voice would carry across the snow, I shouted at my quarry, 'Did you really think I would leave you to be dead? You came after my family. Now I'm coming after you.'

The answer I got in return was a volley of rounds. They smashed into the ground and into headstones all around me as I hunkered to the ground. The snow was soaking through my clothing and penetrating my flesh to chill my bones, but I felt good for the first time in two days. At least one, but probably two or more were hurt, and they had to believe the net was closing in on them.

Amanda's voice broke my train of thought. 'They're in the woods and moving away, Tempest. I sure hope the next part works.'

I did too.

Big Fat Clue

Now that the team were away from us, Big Ben and I ran for the street. We were no more than fifty yards inside the graveyard, the distance covered in a few seconds as we ran bent over - just in case – back to the cars.

Frank and Amanda were monitoring the team as they moved through the woodland behind the cemetery. It extended for a distance of roughly three hundred yards where it reached the M25 motorway. The drones were high above them, following the orange blobs of heat, stark against the cold ground everywhere else. This was the easy bit, now we had to get lucky.

There were several guesses in my plan, but so far, I was on the money.

At the cars, we ducked inside and peeled away, me following Big Ben as we sped back to where we'd left Amanda, Frank, and Dad. They appeared at the mouth of an alleyway, the drone controls in their hands as they continued to monitor the Undead team. Dad was leading them as Amanda and Frank focused on the screens, but they all looked our way as we pulled up.

'They're about to come out of the woods,' Amanda told me as she clambered in. 'They are right by the motorway which is playing havoc with the infrared; there's too much heat coming off the road unless I drop down closer to them.'

We didn't want to tip our hand and have them spot the drones, but if we lost them now, this was all for nothing. I was betting they had cars stashed out of sight not far from the motorway. It would give them a swift getaway with multiple directions to pick from, and they had to pick somewhere tucked out of sight to make sure they weren't seen getting their weapons out.

We would soon know if we were right or not. I called Jane from the car as I set off to intercept them on the motorway.

'Hi, Tempest,' Jane's voice came over the car's speakers. 'Who's with you?'

'Just Amanda,' said Amanda. 'The guys are in the other car.'

'Are you ready?' I asked her.

Jane sounded ready when she replied. 'You bet.'

Amanda dropped the drone lower until she could once again make out the orange blobs moving along the edge of the treeline. They stayed ten yards in as they tracked along parallel to the motorway. They were out of sight to anyone not using thermal imagery, but they couldn't escape us, and soon, we spotted their transport. It looked like two vans. Ford transits maybe. It was hard to determine make and model using the thermal camera but the latent warmth from their engines made them easy to see.

'Are you getting this?' asked Big Ben over the radio. He

was in the car ahead of me with Dad and Frank. All three tried to look innocent as two police cars shot past us on the other side of the road. They were heading to where we had just been; the site of a gun fight that must be drawings cops in from all over. It would keep them busy for a while.

Big Ben was checking we could see the vehicles. They were close to the motorway, about a hundred yards up a path through the woodland that exited right next to a motorway roundabout. In seconds, they would be in the vans and on the three-lane highway.

Which direction they then went, we needed to find out. After that, the drones would lose them, unable to keep pace at motorway speeds, but we had allowed for that.

'I'm switching to standard feed,' announced Frank. I couldn't see his screen but a glance at Amanda's revealed the Undead climbing into their vans. A plume of heat turned the bonnet white as the engine came to life and a second bright spot appeared where the exhaust kicked out. 'They're both new plate Renault Traffic vans. Both dark grey or maybe black,' Frank reported.

'Got that, Jane?' I asked. She was on the phone in my car but could just about hear the voices coming over our radios.

'Sure. That's not much use without a registration number though,' Jane made an obvious statement.

Now it was time to cross our fingers and hope this bit would work. I could see Amanda had her teeth gritted as she flicked the camera from infrared feed to standard and dropped the drone low. We had to get in close to be able to see the numbers and letters in the dark but had to wait until they were in the van or they would see the drones descend. It gave Amanda and Frank a window of a few seconds only. 'I've got the front one, Frank!' she cried triumphantly, clicking a button to take a picture, and tilting the screen to show me.

'I think I ... yes, I've got the rearmost!' Frank called back, excitement making his voice louder than it needed to be.

'Jane!' shouted Amanda. 'Here's the first vehicle registration.' Then she recited it to her, got a verbal thumbs up from Jane and gave her Frank's as well as he recited it into the radio, and she repeated it.

'Give me two minutes!' Jane replied, her voice keeping pace with the general level of enthusiasm.

Would the vans be registered to them? What would she find? We would know soon enough but for now the drones were chasing again, following the vans as they pulled away. Out of the woods, they paused to join the traffic on the roundabout that formed the on and off ramps for both directions of the motorway as it linked the major highway to the local towns and villages.

I held my breath as I waited for Amanda or Frank to announce which way they had gone. If we lost them now, we at least had vehicle registrations we might be able to trace back to something useful. That wasn't the plan though; I wanted to follow them to wherever they were going.

They'd been operating in this area for several days. Maybe longer given that they'd faked Dean's death two months ago now. What was it that had gone wrong this time they pulled the stunt? It was the sixth time they'd killed an innocent and passed them off as one of the team. Each time, it was the wife who made the false identification, but Monica hadn't vanished like the others, she'd come to me instead.

I remembered something. 'Jane, is Monica Moore's social media profile still active?'

I got an, 'Um,' in response. 'I can only do one thing at a time, Tempest, and I'm already doing two. I'll get back to you in a minute, okay?'

'Of course,' I replied, wondering what the other thing might be since she was supposed to be looking for the vehicles' ownership.

'They're going south!' announced Amanda and Frank at almost the same time.

'Land the drones,' I cried, 'We'll pick them up later.' The chase was on. Once on the motorway, there were multiple exits they could pick. We had to catch sight of them fast, just in case they took the next one, and vanished before we could start to tail them.

Ahead of me, Big Ben floored his Land Rover. We were coming out of Swanley but still a minute from the motorway and would be more than a mile behind them when we joined it. Beside me, Amanda was shrugging off the straps for the drone control and twisting to put it on the back seat. I could see Frank doing something similar in the car ahead.

These were tense seconds, but Jane broke them up by announcing she had tracked the vehicles. 'They are both rented,' she told us, 'by a firm called Diphthong Enterprises. I am just looking into them now, but they are not registered at Companies House which probably means they are a dummy firm.'

It was not what I wanted to hear. We needed them to be registered to a name so we could trace it. I was certain the six men all had new identities; getting the name for one might open a whole new line of enquiry that would help us catch them.

'I don't think that matters though,' Jane added. 'I've got something better.'

Her announcement came as we reached the roundabout and were able to power up the on-ramp and onto the motorway. The road was lit and the traffic sparse, which made breaking the speed limit much safer. Big Ben soon had his car doing over a hundred miles per hour with me right on his tail. Assuming the Undead were obeying the seventy limit to not risk drawing attention to themselves, we would catch them in under two minutes.

That was good, but I was more excited to hear what Jane might have to say. 'What have you found?' I asked her, peering through the windscreen at the cars and trucks ahead as I tried to spot the vans.

'The, ah, the email they sent you that hacked your laptop and sent them everything wasn't as clever as they thought. It was designed to look like junk so you would have deleted it without even registering it was there. However, it had a whole program tucked in behind it that then attacked your system. I used the email to track my way back to the computer that sent it.'

'You can do that?' asked Amanda, screwing her face up in disbelief.

Carefully, Jane said, 'There is software that can. The point is, I was able to reverse engineer their program and it is currently sending me everything on their hard drive plus it's sucking data from the cloud backup they use. Shortly, I will have everything.'

My eyes popped out of my head as simultaneously my jaw dropped open and I choked in surprise. 'You'll have everything?'

'Well, everything that exists on their computer,' she corrected her statement. 'It really wasn't that difficult. It makes for interesting reading. I know where the wives are if that's something you would like to know,' she bragged.

'Oh, my God,' uttered Amanda, her voice coming out as barely more than a breath as she and I locked eyes. We had them.

Then Big Ben's voice broke the spell. 'I just spotted them. I'm slowing down.' His brake lights flashed on briefly as he brought the car down to a more sensible speed.

'Where are you going?' I murmured a question I would have to answer myself. Settling in a little more than two hundred yards behind them, I was confident they wouldn't spot us. If they checked their rear view, all they would see was headlights. Snow began to fall again, big white flakes filling the air so it looked like we were on the Millennium Falcon and about to make the jump to hyperspace. It forced all the traffic to slow, the vans and us included.

The motorway led to the southeast coast, terminating at Dover where they could drive straight onto a ferry. They wouldn't risk taking the guns with them, at least I didn't think they would, but there were lots of other destinations they might have in mind. Tailing them along the straight road, I had Jane lay out what she'd already found.

'The wives are in Malta,' she revealed. 'You remember seeing the email with the picture of a yacht on it?'

'Yeah.'

'Well, the yacht is registered there, and they have more than one between them. It was purchased new from Sunseekers Yachts two years ago for a price of nearly three million pounds.' A memory of seeing a Sunseekers cata- logue in the pile of mail in Rob McTavish's house surfaced. He'd been browsing and getting excited about the new life he was going to.

Amanda whistled at the figure. 'There's no sign that

they have that kind of money. You said Rob McTavish's house in Scotland was average,' she reminded me.

I nodded my head. 'It is. I got no sense that he had money, but he did have a catalogue for Sunseeker yachts in his mail.'

'Ah,' said Jane, cutting in. 'I think I can explain where the money came from.'

I waited for her to tell us, but she was clearly waiting for me to tell her to go ahead. 'We're all ears,' I said to get her talking.

'It's Iraqi gold.' The words hit me like a wave breaking over my brain. That had to be what the investigation was about.

'They robbed a bank in Iraq?' Amanda asked.

I shook my head. 'Most likely it was one of Saddam Hussein's palaces or weekend retreats. I went into one of them once the war fighting part was over. Everything was gold from the taps in the sink, to the handles on the wardrobes, and these guys were some of the first to get into the country. They found gold and they probably killed a bunch of Iraqi soldiers to get it. I bet they found a way to smuggle it out but got caught after the fact. Investigators would have traced the rounds in the Iraqi soldier's bodies and matched them to the guns but there would be no way to disprove whatever story they came up with. They attacked an enemy stronghold and killed the combatants inside: that's completely legal. However, they were suspected of stealing a load of gold, and though it was never proven, they were drummed out of the unit anyway. Then they had to bide their time.'

'For how long?' asked Jane. 'How long until the case would be dropped or forgotten about?'

Amanda replied, 'For missing gold? The investigation would never be closed.'

I nodded along. 'Their only option was to disappear. They couldn't just up and go though, they needed to make the investigation team, or whoever might be keeping tabs, believe they were dead. The six of them cooked the whole thing up and were patient enough and wise enough to wait a decade and then do it slowly, one at a time with pauses in between. Slowly, they moved to a new place, the value of the gold they stole augmented by hefty insurance pay outs, and whatever else they could get their hands on.'

'Like Dean Moore stealing all the profit from his own firm and taking out loans he never intended to repay,' added Amanda.

'And his wife, Monica ripping off his business partner,' said Jane.

Her comment made me think about my client for the first time in a few hours and it made me frown with doubt. 'I think that's different.'

Amanda gave me a quizzical look. 'How so?'

'I think she sold the firm to Evan Allcorn and ripped him off because she knew if he were the sole owner, the banks would go to him alone to recover their debt. If she took over her husband's shares, then she was equally liable.'

'But wasn't she the one who falsely identified Dean's body?' asked Jane. 'I don't get it. She's in on it, so why would she care about the bank coming for the money if she's planning to vanish with her husband? Rip off Evan, I get that bit, but how is this different from scamming the insurance firm?'

A picture was starting to form in my head. It was something I'd considered and rejected already, but it was starting to make sense now. 'What if you wanted to end a relationship but you couldn't because you were complicit in a crime? The moment Monica Moore failed to report what her husband was up to, which is way back whenever he first revealed the big plan, she tied herself to him. Imagine if you were through with a marriage but couldn't escape. All six wives are still with their husbands almost twenty years after we knew them. That defies the statistics. If we assume Monica wanted out, she has to wait for him to fake his own death. Maybe she'd been planning it for years, maybe she only decided after he was buried and discovered she preferred life without him. Either way, she gets the money and doesn't go to join him. Instead, she hires me. I'm guessing this bit, but I think Dean Moore had seen me on the news recently and made a comment about knowing me. It gave her an idea.'

'They're turning off,' Big Ben's voice crackled over the radio.

I peered through the snow to see a blinking indicator on both vans. A glance at the road sign showed that we were close to Ashford. They were not heading for the port of Dover unless they planned to make a pitstop first. Now it became trickier to tail them because our headlights would make us highly visible. Once off the motorway, we were in rural countryside with very little around us and zero cars – we would look suspicious in their rear view.

'I'm going dark,' I announced into the radio.

I got a, 'Roger,' in return and Big Ben's Land Rover all but vanished as he turned off his lights. I did the same, relying on the snow to give us enough see by. It worked perfectly but only because of the snow. Where the road had been gritted, it was clear; a black line bordered by white on either side. We kept our distance and kept going.

'What was the idea?' asked Amanda, prompting me to continue my hypothesis.

'This is all conjecture,' I reminded her. 'Jane, did you get to check Monica's social media yet?' I asked her.

I heard her tut. 'Sorry, I clean forgot. Delving into the Undead Incorporated's computer files distracted me. Hold on.' There were a few seconds of nothing before she spoke again. 'It's still there. There are no recent posts, but unlike the others, it hasn't been wiped. I'm going to poke around a bit and see what I can find.'

I continued with my theory about the client. 'For whatever reason, she didn't vanish the way she was supposed to. She ripped off Evan Allcorn and pooled the money she had. Dean is sighted in the area because he is in the area. He came back to get her or to find out why she hadn't come to him. I'm going to guess that once he was officially dead, she begged him to let her go. That wasn't part of the plan though and he didn't like it. He came back and she came to me. She knew that I was at the same unit as him and probably thought that meant I was also SOS.'

'It's an easy mistake to make,' said Amanda. 'I didn't understand the difference.

'She would have, but it was a long time ago and I never met her back then. She hired me to investigate her husband. Maybe she thought me poking around would scare him off. Perhaps she hoped my involvement would draw their attention.'

'Which it did,' Jane commented.

'Which it did,' I echoed. 'She would certainly have expected their attention to switch from her to me and that might give her the chance to escape. She was being tailed by a team of former special forces soldiers and needed some free space to get away. Maybe she had a plan, but Ponytail turned up and I got into a fight with him. She knew the police would show up and she decided to go early. She could be in Cuba now for all I know.'

'They're turning again,' said Big Ben. 'They must be closing in on where they are going. There's not a whole lot out here.'

'Oh, yes there is,' I argued. 'We just passed a sign with a picture of an airplane on it. We're out near Jukeston airstrip.'

Big Ben sounded doubtful, 'Never heard of it.'

'I doubt many people have. I only know of it because one of my early cases was looking into a ghostly Spitfire.'

'Cor, yeah, I remember that one,' chuckled Frank.

I continued to explain. 'It turned out to be a publicity stunt in the lead up to the D-Day anniversary celebrations, but I went to the airfield. It's a small, members-only place for enthusiasts. I'm willing to bet these guys have a light plane here and they plan to escape on it.'

'You can't fly a small aircraft from England to Malta,' argued my dad.

'They don't need to,' I pointed out. 'They just need to get out of the country. They can land in France or Spain and get to Malta in bounds. I'm betting they have fake passports and can board a commercial jet if they so choose. They have wounded though, and they have weapons to carry.'

'I'm calling for backup,' said Amanda, grimacing at the thought of calling Chief Inspector Quinn.

'They just made the turning,' Big Ben let us know. 'Do we follow?'

Sneak Attack

While Amanda dialled the number on her phone to speak with her former boss, Ian Quinn, I thought about our options. They were still armed, but they were also going to escape if we didn't try to stop them.

After a few seconds of indecision, I said, 'I don't think we have a choice, Ben.'

'Let's get 'em,' growled my dad, thinking heroic thoughts and not considering the danger.

I blew out a worried breath and exchanged a glance with Amanda. She looked as concerned as I felt, but the phone was ringing and before we could speak, Chief Inspector Quinn answered it.

'Miss Harper. To what do I owe the pleasure this evening?' he sneered at her. I'd really pissed him off earlier.

She shot me a look: she wanted me to talk to him. 'Ian, it's Tempest. We have the evidence, we have the team, and we know what it is all about. If you want a fat feather for your cap, you are going to have to scramble everything you can get to Jukeston airstrip. They are planning to fly out of here and once they are gone, it's going to be a lot harder to get them back.'

He didn't answer straight away, but there was a change in tone on the line. Amanda whispered, 'He just put you on speaker so other officers can hear.'

'These are the men you claim are responsible for the car bomb this morning and for the shooting last night?' he asked.

'Exactly right. Look, Ian, we have no time to discuss this. They just shot up a graveyard in Swanley but now they are here, and they are armed. I am going in but I'm not sure what we can do to stop them escaping.'

'Horsten cemetery in Swanley?' he repeated. 'That is your work? I think there may be some questions for you to answer, Mr Michaels. It would seem shots were fired in more than one direction this time. Are you armed?'

I sighed and wished I hadn't let the bit about Swanley slip, but it was too late now. 'Ian, I'm ending the call. Get your tactical team here as fast as you can and earn a great collar. Or don't, the choice is yours. If I'm still alive when you arrive, I'll tell you about Swanley.' I nodded at Amanda who jabbed the red button to end the call as if she were jabbing Quinn in the eye.

'I truly loathe that man,' she moaned.

'He can be a little irritating,' I agreed. 'We may need to ditch Frank's weapons before they arrive,' I voiced my thoughts out loud.

Frank heard me, his voice coming back over the radio. 'But they're replicas of Lara Croft's handguns from *Tomb Raider*,' he complained. 'They weren't easy to come by, I'll have you know.'

'We could still go to jail for using them,' Amanda pointed out.

Frank changed his mind. 'I can buy new ones.'

Ahead of us, as we closed to within a hundred yards of the two vans, the lead vehicle's headlights illuminated a building.

'What is this place?' asked Amanda, squinting into the dark.

'An old second world war short range fighter aircraft take-off and landing strip originally. It was flat land close to the coast. Since then, they've built a bigger control tower and added some other buildings.'

'That looks like commercial units,' she pointed out.

Just ahead of us Big Ben coasted to a stop, using the gearbox and little else to get the vehicle to stop so the brake lights wouldn't flare and show the Undead we were right behind them.

'Do you think they know we are here?' she asked with a nervous tremor.

I pulled the handbrake on and killed the engine. 'No. They'd have led us somewhere remote and shot at us by now if they did. Jane?'

'Yes,'

'We're leaving the car now. Send something juicy from the evidence you already have to CI Quinn, please. That should get things moving. Maybe give him the addresses they have in Malta and something to do with the gold.'

'Okay, Tempest. Guys?' she stopped us just as we were getting out of the car. 'Be careful, okay?'

I didn't make any daft promises about not having to worry. Worry was definitely the right emotion to go with. Instead, I thanked her for her help on the case and told her to keep going with what she was doing.

We were more than a hundred yards behind them and mostly hidden by a line of trees that flanked the road on either side. The road was little more than compressed gravel and it led only from the B road behind us to the airfield itself. We'd left enough room for the police to squeeze by, assuming they got here in time, and now we were gathered in a gaggle to discuss our next move.

'How quickly can a person get an aircraft started and into the air?' asked Amanda.

I shrugged. I didn't know the answer to that question, but I felt sure it wasn't a lot of time. I guessed at, 'Not long enough for armed police to get here. What weapons have we got?'

'Not enough,' said Big Ben. 'We should have brought Frank's matching bazookas.'

'I don't have a bazooka,' Frank pointed out. 'Let alone matching ones.'

Big Ben looked down at him. 'Well, there is a lesson to learn there, Frank. More bazookas required. Stop buying magical sickles crafted by Smurfs to ward off pixies.'

'Smurfs aren't real,' grumped Frank, annoyed that Big Ben never took him seriously.

While Big Ben was playing the fool, Amanda and my father had laid out what weapons we had in the boot of the lead Land Rover. Dad listed them: 'Two small calibre hand-guns, two swords, what did you bring those for?' he asked me with genuine curiosity.

'I put them in,' said Frank. 'They are too cool be left behind.'

Frank got a single raised eyebrow from my father. 'Righto. What else? One illumination round, a bow and some arrows with various heads, one of which is explosive, and that's about it.'

It wasn't a lot. 'Chances are our adversaries are armed to the teeth.' I was ready to wager they were loaded to take on a small army if it came to it. 'We only need to stop them from escaping in their aircraft. Big Ben and I will take the handguns and sneak up to them. When we know which plane is theirs, we'll put some holes in it. We can do it once they are on board to minimise any danger.'

'I don't like it, Tempest. Can't we wait? If they get away, it sounds like the evidence Jane has will be enough to get Interpol to make the arrests.'

'Maybe,' I couldn't fault her logic. 'But we don't know if they have fall back positions in place. They get a sniff that we have hacked their computer, and they go into the wind again. They've faked their own deaths once. They could do it again and then we all spend our lives looking over our shoulders and wondering what might happen when we put the key in the ignition of our cars.' Her car exploding this morning was a fresh and terrible memory for both of us and enough to stop her from arguing any further.

'Stay on the radio,' Dad insisted.

With a promise to do just that, Big Ben and I snuck into the dark. I paused only briefly to get my hands under the snow and into the dirt. It was almost frozen solid, but I got enough muck on my hands to be able to darken my face. I nudged Big Ben who followed suit.

It took only a minute to cover the ground to the parked vans. They were abandoning them here, they no longer needed them, but they were taking their weapons. Or rather they were trying to. I couldn't tell who from the team was missing, not right away, but as we got closer, I saw why I could only see three of them. One was sitting on the ground, a field dressing on his chest on which I could see dark stains. He was wounded and it looked to be Rob McTavish. He'd aged a lot since I last saw him, more so in the last hour as his blood drained away. They didn't have the option of getting medical help, much the same as getting injured on any other covert op, but from his pallor, I wasn't sure Rob was going to make it to wherever they were going.

Now that we were close enough to see their faces, I could make out Beefy and Vince Barnes. Their racial heritage made them easy to recognise. Also visible was Edgar Salter, his ginger hair going grey at the sides but still bright orange enough to stand out. Where did that put Dean and Martin?

When a voice in my head whispered, 'They're behind you,' I spun around, paranoia driving me to check my six.

Big Ben nudged my arm and pointed away to our left. Two flashlights were moving about on the airfield. 'They are split up,' he pointed out. 'They also have no idea we are here. We can take them.'

'Bad idea,' I hissed. 'We should wait until these guys move forward to the plane. Once they are on board, we can cripple it.'

'We can try to cripple it,' he argued. 'What if we put a dozen holes in it but they take off anyway?'

We both knew he was right. But before we needed to make a decision Edgar keeled over. Rob McTavish wasn't the only one hurt: I had heard two separate cries of pain earlier. Beefy and Vince began arguing. It looked like Vince wanted to abandon them and Beefy wanted him to help carry their wounded comrades to the plane.

'This might be our chance,' whispered Big Ben.

They were distracted, that was what Big Ben meant but the moment we broke out from the treeline we were hidden in, they would see us. Did they have their weapons slung to their bodies? I couldn't see in the dark, not from this distance. They weren't in their hands but that didn't mean they couldn't return fire before we got to them. I didn't want a shootout. If we killed them, there would be trouble, and if they shot at us and missed, my father, my girlfriend, and the crazy guy from the bookshop were directly behind us. At the very least, we would need to move position and come at them from a different angle if we did attack.

They were kind enough to give us a third option. Beefy jabbed Vince in the chest and shouted him down. Vince wasn't happy about it, but he begrudgingly hauled Rob McTavish from the floor and into a fireman's carry. Rob cried out in pain and got a barbed retort and threat back from Vince who then started across the field in the direction of the flashlights. Beefy hauled Edgar onto his own shoulders and followed.

They might still have their weapons, but they couldn't get to them easily now they were carrying their friends.

Big Ben slapped my arm; he was going. As he powered out of the trees, I was right on his shoulder. We both had our Lara Croft handguns, but I didn't think we would have to fire them.

We ran silently, crossing the field swiftly as we closed the distance. I pointed to Vince's back. I was going to run straight through him and expected Big Ben to do the same to Beefy, but Rob McTavish lifted his head when we were still ten metres away and he screamed blue murder.

'Ambush!' It was all he needed to say to make Beefy and Vince react, and their reaction was instant. Hardwired responses honed by years of training and staying alive in dangerous environments caused them to drop the casualties.

Rob screamed as he fell to the ground and again as he hit it. There was no noise at all from Edgar, who could be dead for all I knew, but with five metres to go, both Beefy and Vince were dropping into a kneeling firing position, making themselves into smaller targets as they brought their weapons around from their backs and up to their shoulders.

Would I get there before he lined up the shot? I just couldn't tell, but I had no way to avoid finding out. With my right arm held out in front of my face, I pulled the trigger on the handgun and threw myself in the air. The shot missed, though I didn't see by how much, and as Vince's assault rifle began to spew rounds, I slammed into him, the bullets passing harmlessly under my left arm as I tackled him to the ground.

The roar of the guns had deafened me, but it was all about the fight now. We were going to win and live or lose and die, there was no third choice.

I caught the scent of burning cotton as the muzzle of his gun dug against my clothing. More shots rang out, his gun expending ammunition into the air as we fought. I wanted to get my gun around to shoot him, but it was pinned, and as he bucked against me, it came loose from my hand.

With no other weapon, I punched him hard in the head and turned my arm so I could strike at him with my elbow. This was close quarters desperate fighting. He could pull a knife at any second and the first thing I would know was when it plunged through my ribs. Yet I couldn't push away to give myself distance because he still had the assault rifle.

His head ground against mine painfully when he ducked my next blow. Getting in close to me took the energy from my swings, that being his intention, but then he snapped out with his skull to hit my jaw, and the taste of blood filled my mouth.

My left arm wrapped around his weapon, nullifying his ability to shoot me with it, but when I tried to get my right arm around his neck, he got a knee up and kicked away. He broke free, my grip on his weapon breaking as he went one way and I went the other.

'This is why you were just the mechanic,' he snarled. His weapon was coming up again and there was no way I could avoid it this time. Halfway up, as he raised the ugly black assault rifle toward me, it started spitting bullets again until inexplicably, it stopped, and so did he, blinking twice before he pitched forward onto his face.

Standing behind him was Big Ben. He was bloodied, a trickle of it running from his mouth and from a cut to his right cheek. Yet in his hands he held Beefy's weapon which he'd used as a club on Vince's skull.

I sucked in a deep lungful of freezing cold air, stunned that I was still alive. Big Ben dropped the gun and offered me a hand up, but we both froze when we heard the engine on the aircraft burst into life.

Warned by the gunfire, Dean and Martin were making good their escape. In the time it took me to get to my feet, the plane was moving, heading for the dark field to take off.

'The vans!' I yelled, starting to run back the way we had come. The plane was moving, and it wouldn't need much runway to get up to flight speed. Our only hope was to get in its way or run into it.

The keys were in the ignition, Big Ben diving in through the passenger door a heartbeat after I threw it into gear and mashed the accelerator. There was no need for subtlety now; they knew we were here, and it was a straight race to see if we could get to them before they got airborne.

Headlights appeared behind me, making me twitch my eyes toward the mirror.

'I think it's ours!' Big Ben yelled, meaning Dad, Frank, and Amanda.

They were way behind us so if we couldn't get to the plane, neither could they.

And I didn't think we could. We were chasing the aircraft and gaining on it, but as it picked up speed, so the amount we gained got less and less. Ahead was a dark mass of trees: the end of the runway, but they would be in the air before they got to it. We were tantalisingly close, no more than two yards from its tail. All I needed was to give it a nudge, but as I closed another inch its wheels left the ground.

I screamed in rage and begged the van to leap forward, but the plane lifted into the air, soaring up into the cloud-filled night sky with no regard for my thoughts.

Watching the last two members of the Undead escape, and cursing the sky, I was shocked to see the tail section of the plane explode.

Escape and Evasion

The plane faltered, stalled, and then fell from the sky, vanishing over the treetops ahead but reporting back a loud crash mere moments later.

I shouted a warning to Big Ben and slammed on the brakes. The Land Rover, with Frank peering over the wheel, appeared alongside us braking equally hard to stop before we both ploughed into the trees. Hanging out of the sunroof and looking demented as the wind whipped his hair around, was my father, the bow tumbling from his right hand as he tried to hold on.

Slewing to a stop on the snow, I looked up at dad and got a bonkers grin in return. 'Was that you?' I shouted.

He brought his hands together and burst them apart with an accompanying boom noise followed by an insane giggle. He used the second exploding arrow to bring the aircraft down.

'Didn't you hear me warn you?' he asked. 'I kept telling you to get out of the way in case it bounced off or I missed.'

I hadn't heard him. Come to think of it, I hadn't heard

anything on the radio at all. Touching my ear, I found the radio to be missing. It had been knocked clear while I fought with Vince, so I hadn't heard any messages from anyone.

Amanda had forced them to drop her off at the scene of our fight. She was securing the four members of Undead Incorporated lying in the snow. To be fair, two were unconscious courtesy of Big Ben, one was very possibly dead, and Rob McTavish hadn't been able to add to the fight against Big Ben and me, so I doubted he was going to give her much trouble now. She was my girlfriend, so I worried about her, but she was also a former police officer and quite able to handle herself.

Using Frank's radio, I asked how she was getting on.

'I'm fine, Tempest. I'm just half frozen. I need a glass of prosecco and a hot bath. Did I see the plane come down? Are they dead?'

Good question. 'Yes, the plane came down. It crash landed in the trees somewhere just ahead of us. Maybe a couple of hundred yards. I wouldn't bet on them being dead though. It wasn't going all that fast, I think they probably got out unharmed.'

'You're not going after them, are you?' she begged.

'No, babe,' I lied.

She saw right through me, of course. 'Do you even have a weapon? There are guns here. I made a pile of them.'

I thought about going back for them but then considered how much the radius of our search would increase with each passing minute that we were not pursuing them. If we hurried, Big Ben and I might get to the plane before they got out. Wasting minutes going back for the guns wasn't an option.

'I've got dad's bow and some arrows,' I told her.

Dad made an awkward noise, bringing my eyes around to look at the two pieces of bow in his hands. 'I think we ran it over when I dropped it,' he said apologetically. 'There are still some arrows,' he suggested hopefully.

Big Ben sniggered. 'Yeah, we can ask them to impale themselves.'

'Do you still have your pistol?' I asked him.

He shook his head. 'Beefy knocked it from my hand, I didn't see where it went, then I had to rescue you, and after that we were chasing a plane.'

'Amanda, I'll be careful. The police must be on their way. I think Edgar is in a bad way, Rob McTavish too, but try to keep them alive. I'm sending Dad and Frank back to you now. I don't think the last two are armed. It will be a straight up fight, and I've got Big Ben with me.'

Big Ben shined his knuckles on his jacket.

'What if they are armed?' she asked.

'Then you'd better take these,' said Frank, stepping forward with the two stupid flaming swords. They weren't lit, and they wouldn't be much use if Dean and Martin had guns, but they were better than nothing.

With a wry smile, I accepted the offered sword. 'Thanks, Frank. We'll see you in a few minutes.'

Dad grabbed me and pulled me into an unexpected hug. He held me for a two count, then slapped my back. 'Stay safe, kiddo.'

Big Ben tugged my arm. 'Let's go.'

We ran into the woods, aiming for the general area where we saw the plane go down. I believed we would find it, but whether we would find the last two members of the Undead team was a different task altogether. The SOS undergo all manner of training, and one element is called escape and evasion. They get dropped off in a remote area with nothing in their pockets and a company of infantry an hour behind them. The simple task is to stay ahead of the pretend enemy. The infantry company has one aim: catch the SOS guys. It is a famous exercise that lives in legend because some of the chaps were so good at it that three weeks later, they would send a postcode from Bondi Beach in Australia having started off in a glen in Scotland.

Now two of us, armed with stupid prop swords, had to try to catch two men who were trained in how to not get caught.

We stayed in sight of each other, but not too close. If we were next to each other and they were armed, one burst from an automatic weapon could kill us both. Moving swiftly to cover the ground, we were soon coming close to the area I expected the find the plane. A metallic noise to our right drew our attention. The plane was that way. In the dark, and moving across undulating land, we'd drifted off course and almost missed it.

Swinging around to face the direction the sound came from, Big Ben reached around my head to clamp a hand over my mouth. Then he pointed with one finger.

I followed it, squinting into the dark until I picked up what he had seen: two dark figures silhouetted against the snow. They were moving through the trees, appearing, and disappearing each time they passed one. Their path was not one that would bring them to us, but we could move to intercept.

Just as I began to move in their direction, Big Ben grabbed my arm and whispered, 'What's the magic word for this thing again?'

'The sword? It's not magic dummy. Frank was being theatrical. All you have to do it press the button on the pommel.'

I tried to move away again, but he had another question. 'What if I want to be theatrical?'

I rolled my eyes. 'It's Incendius, okay? Don't forget to do the flourish with your hand,' I joked.

'Oh, yeah!' he gasped. 'I'd forgotten about that. Hey, we should do it together.'

'What?'

'We get ahead of them, then step out from behind two trees, say the magic word with a flourish and watch them mess their pants when our magic swords spring to life.' He was totally serious.

The sensible thing to do would be argue or perhaps point out that they might shoot us both while we played with our swords, but I didn't have a better plan. 'Okay, Ben. Let's try that.'

Getting ahead of them without them seeing us coming, wasn't easy. Or, more accurately, it wasn't quick. It required us to take a wide berth so they wouldn't see us as we navigated around to get in front of the path they were on. The difficult part lay in that we couldn't get too far away from them, or we might lose them completely in the dark wood. Luck, judgement, and the two men not bothering to move stealthily enabled us to arrive, several minutes later, behind two large tree trunks. They were about five yards apart and it looked like Dean and Martin were going to pass between them.

I let Big Ben count it down as they approached. His voice came through my earpiece, 'Three, two, one.'

In a single motion, we both stepped out from behind the trees to block their path and said aloud, 'Incendius.' With a swish of our hands, the flame leapt up the blade of our swords to illuminate the immediate area.

We must have looked hellish because Martin screamed

and Dean fled, breaking right, and running through the trees for all he was worth. I saw Big Ben give chase, the flame from his sword fluttering behind him as he charged through the dark woods after his quarry. 'I've got Dean!' I yelled as I chased after him. Neither man had drawn a weapon, which had to mean they didn't have any. That's what I told myself as I ran through the dark.

Old brambles tore at my clothes and the flame from the sword messed with my night vision no matter where I held it. Dean was only a few yards ahead of me though, and I knew I was going to catch him unless I fell over an unseen obstacle.

It looked lighter ahead, and chasing after him, I realised we were heading for a clearing. He burst from the trees first, losing a little height as the ground dipped away slightly.

I shouted, 'Stop, Dean! There's nowhere for you to go.'

He slowed and spun around to face me. 'There's always somewhere to go,' he growled. We were facing off, my flaming sword held up by my head and ready should he be foolish enough to charge me. The flames showed me his face and he looked calm. Watching him to see what he would do, and in no hurry as time was on my side, not his, I got to see him reach inside his tactical vest and produce a machete. Its blade gleamed wickedly in the dancing light coming from my sword.

'Think you can beat me, do you? I told you right at the start that we were better than you. You got lucky, but here's where your luck runs out.' I let him talk; he was just killing time he couldn't afford to lose. 'Do you even know how to use a sword?' he asked. 'Ever fought with one?'

My mind skipped back to a battle in a house in Cawsand. I'd barely survived the encounter, but the answer was still a confident, 'Yes. I have, actually. And I won.'

He sneered back at me. 'You hold tight to that memory while I'm cutting out your heart, Tempest Michaels. Who are you to come after my team?'

'You disgraced your unit,' I fired back at him. 'You murdered and stole, and you've been murdering and stealing ever since. Who are you to think you have a right to freedom?'

All the while we were talking, we were circling each other. The clearing was a small lake, I'd realised once I got a chance to look at it. The perfectly flat white surface couldn't be anything else. It had frozen over in the recent cold and was now covered in snow. The ice wouldn't be thick though, not thick enough to support a man I thought until Dean stepped onto it and proved me wrong.

'What's the matter, boy? You don't want to follow me out onto the ice? Afraid you might get wet? In the toughest conditions, that's where we thrive. That you pause to question the danger is why you could never be like me. You could never have succeeded in my environment.' What he said was true. I wasn't cut out to undergo the level of training he'd put himself through to qualify to wear their capbadge, but I didn't feel bad about it because almost no one on the planet meets the mark. Over ninety percent of applicants fail the selection course. However, none of that had any bearing on our current situation.

'What happened with Monica?' I asked him like we were having a pleasant conversation. When I got no answer, I badgered him. 'Come on. You're planning to gut me, aren't you? Why not reveal the truth behind the mystery I've been trying to solve? Did she have a change of heart?'

I didn't think for one second that he would answer my question, so it came as a surprise when he started talking. 'She fell out with the other girls. They were all sunning it up in Malta and spending money on yachts, jewels, and champagne while she was still working a job. This was always the plan. I would go last. It was my team, so it was my job to let them go before me.' I recognised his feelings on the matter; it was a standard army thing: the boss always eats last. Not first, the way civilians seem to do it, worshipping the CEO because he demands it. 'Monica just got so fed up with it and we argued all the time. She wanted kids, that was part of it, but we all agreed that taking kids with us, making them vanish too, would be too much to ask. They would talk and we would all get caught.' He sounded melancholy instead of murderous for a moment, but the deadly side of Dean wasn't gone for long. 'Right then. Shall we get to the killing bit. It's quite cool out tonight and I need to get moving along.'

I'd told myself to be ready for the lunge or charge when it came but I wasn't. Not really. He screamed a war cry and darted forward, raising the machete high above his head to swing it back down at my head as he leapt from the ground.

I saw the blow coming and swept my flaming sword up to parry it away. There was no clang of metal on metal though. Unlike his blade, mine was intended to look pretty, so when his struck mine, it snapped it in half. The top half of my sword spun away into the darkness but the exposed gas pipe running up the centre of the hollow shaft ignited instantly to shoot a gout of flame into Dean's face.

His scream was inhuman in both volume and pitch. We were right at the edge of the lake. He had one foot on the ice and the other on the land, but in my fight or flight reaction to the sword breaking, I kicked out with my right foot, landing a blow to his chest that drove him backwards even as he was reeling from his facial burns. He fell, his arms going out to his sides as he hit the ice and smashed through it.

I dropped my useless sword. What was left of it anyway. All the gas had gone up in one final blast when his machete cleaved it into two pieces, ruining my night vision and leaving a bright corona in front of both eyes. Struggling to see, I could still tell that Dean had gone under the ice. I waded in after him, gritting my teeth against the terrible bite of the ice-cold water. The ice was thicker than I expected, maybe half an inch or more I discovered. His body had broken it, but his momentum carried him onward, under the unbroken portion. He was down there now, running out of air and unable to find his way back to the hole.

There was a part of me that insisted going under the ice to find him was the right thing to do. Ultimately, though, it wasn't the probability of dying myself that stopped me from trying to rescue him, it was his own advice: leave the dead to be dead.

On frozen feet, I staggered back out of the water. I felt like collapsing as the weight of the last three days washed away to leave me feeling exhausted. It was done. The team were down, the mystery was solved, and the case could be closed. My part in this was over, and the police would be here soon. Thinking about the police, I told myself to head back to the airfield. They would need someone to lead them in.

It was then that I realised I was lost.

A Story to Tell

It took more than five hours for the police to find me, by which time hypothermia was winning its battle to lower my core temperature. My radio was either out of range or its battery had died. It didn't matter which because the end result was the same. With no way to communicate with anyone since I'd stupidly left my phone in the car, I knew the safest thing to do was wait in one spot. People would search for me, and I felt confident I would be found because my general area was known. It turned out they had a really good idea where to look because Big Ben was with them. He'd caught and overpowered Martin Kemp in seconds, knocking him out before carrying him back to the edge of the airstrip. He expected me to find him there, setting out to search for me when I failed to appear. He continued searching and calling for me until the police arrived, then joined in with them, as did Amanda, Frank, and my father.

They were searching expanding grids from the plane. Unfortunately, I wasn't anywhere near the plane. In chasing Dean, I'd covered more than three hundred yards which is why it took them so long to find me. I'd exercised to keep myself warm, but I'd needed more layers and it didn't help that I was wet up to my upper thighs.

I fell asleep in the ambulance being warmed with heated blankets while a worried Amanda tried to hide her concern. I didn't fight the medical treatment; I like to think I am bright enough to know when I need it, and this was one of those occasions.

Amanda left me at the hospital and took a taxi home. Her home that is, not mine or Frank's or anyone else's. The danger was gone; there would be no more car bombs. This case had cost her a car. Insurance would pay for it, but with a sly grin as I fell back to sleep, I realised I'd just worked out what to give her for Christmas.

At 1515hrs that afternoon, waiting impatiently to be discharged and chatting with Amanda, Chief Inspector Quinn knocked on the door to my room and let himself in. 'Good afternoon, Miss Harper, Mr Michaels. I trust you are feeling recovered.'

'I'm fine, thank you, Ian,' I replied. I was curious to hear why he was visiting but waited for him to get to it.

'You may wish to know that Dean Moore's body was recovered a few hours ago. Police divers found it under the ice as you said. The other injured persons have all survived and look likely to recover from their wounds. They can expect long jail sentences; the type that never actually end. Application has been made to exhume all the graves to see just who was buried in each case.'

'What of the wives?' I asked.

'Ah, yes,' he commented brightly as if my question led him neatly to his next point. 'I had to push that one up the chain. Arranging the arrest of persons and the seizure of property in another country is a little beyond my current bounds. However, I am assured the arrests were made late this morning. The evidence James Butterworth supplied,' the chief inspector knew my petite blonde detective was a man and refused to refer to him as anything other than the name on his birth certificate, 'proved to be convincingly thorough. The computer forensics team will be sifting it for some time, I am sure.'

'What of the gold?' asked Amanda. 'It was stolen from Iraq, was it not? Will it be returned to the Iraqi people?'

The chief inspector gave her a curious look. 'That is well above my pay grade to decide, Miss Harper. However, I imagine that whatever happens to any gold that is left, and whatever assets can be recovered, nothing will be given to anyone until after the trial of the suspects.' He turned his attention to me. 'There is one other person in all this about whom you have yet to ask me.'

Sitting up straighter in my chair next to the bed, I pursed my lips. 'Monica Moore? Do you know what happened to her?'

'Indeed,' he replied. 'I have her in custody. We found her in the wreckage of the plane. She was lucky to be alive given that the plane fell from the sky and she wasn't strapped in. She was handcuffed and gagged and fitted with a hood so she couldn't see. According to Mrs Moore, her husband had kidnapped her from their home three days ago.'

My mind did the math. It must have happened right when Big Ben and I were fighting Ponytail outside her house. 'You have her in custody?' I tried to clarify.

Ian smiled. 'Yes. She might be telling the truth about getting kidnapped, but I feel certain that her claim to know nothing about the gold, the murders, or her husband faking his death will all prove to be lies.' He studied my face for a moment while I let the information sink in. 'I do hope you got paid up front, Mr Michaels.'

He was back to being a dick to me and I kinda liked it. It let me know where I stood. A smile broke out on my face. I wasn't getting paid, but it really didn't matter. The firm would manage just fine, and it was Christmas in two days – a time for celebration and relaxation.

Sensing that the conversation was over, Quinn stood up, dusted some lint from his cap and moved to the door. With his right hand on the handle, he paused and turned back to face me. 'Oh, I almost forgot. Two handguns were recovered from the airfield. The prints on them don't match those of the five men we have in custody. Nor do they match Dean Moore. I think I will, however, find the ballistics report matches bullets recovered from Horsten cemetery in Swanley. You wouldn't like to shed any light on that, would you, Mr Michaels?'

I kept my face completely emotionless.

He nodded. 'I thought not. I find myself wondering if I might find the prints matched yours or Mr Winters. Kindly see to it that I don't find a good reason to check. There's a good fellow.' It was a warning, a friendly one which he didn't have to give me. Firearms charges, given what happened this week and how we brought the criminals to justice, might be successfully fought, but the wrong judge might see things differently and choose to put me and Big Ben away for a spell.

I thought he was done, but he paused one last time on his way out of the door. 'Please have Mr Butterworth contact my computer forensics team. They have some questions about the files he sent over but reported to me earlier that he is not answering his phone.'

'She,' I made a point of specifying Jane's preferred

gender, 'is probably asleep. We all pulled some long hours this week.'

'Ah,' he smiled. 'That might explain the music playing when his phone connects then.' He let the door swing closed and we were alone again.

Neither of us said anything for a few seconds, then we looked at each other, both frowning in confusion. 'Music?' Amanda repeated the chief inspector's word. 'What music?'

I had my phone out and was calling her number. It rang and rang but just when I thought it was going to connect to the voicemail service, it was answered.

Except it wasn't. No one spoke, but a piece of music started playing and it chilled my blood to recognise the happy, chirpy tones of the Chordettes as they sang Mr Sandman.

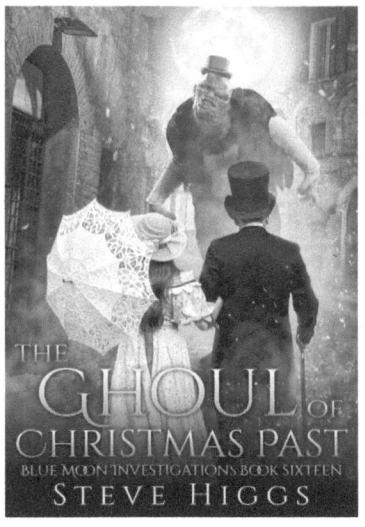

vinci-books.com/ghoul-christmaspast

A theft from a museum, a missing man, and a scary figure lurking in the shadows... what do they add up to?

Twas the day before Christmas and Michael Michaels is about to upset his wife. Recent adventures with his son, Tempest, have piqued his need for a little more action in his life... but when he finds himself facing off against a giant ghoul a few hours later, he begins to think he should have listened to Mary and stayed at home.

Turn the page for a free preview...

The Ghoul of Christmas Past: Chapter One

THE GHOUL

Saturday, December 24th 0615hrs

The sense that he was being watched crept over him as he left his house in the predawn gloom. Jason Pendergrass was one of those lucky people who was born into money. He'd never worked, not really. His great-grandfather made the family fortune with an engineering firm he started. In the beginning, it made buttons, of all things, but at the advent of the Second World War, he secured funding to convert the factory to produce bullets and later components for armoured vehicles.

Selling over-priced parts that could not be obtained elsewhere proved to be highly lucrative, most especially when Jason's own father spotted the trend toward computerised components and plugged a whole pile of money into R&D. Now they led the market in thermal imagery and targeting equipment and he couldn't spend all he had coming in even if he tried.

His father forced him to learn the business and take a job on the board, but ironically, it bored him. Less than a week after his father's untimely death, Jason stepped down and focussed on doing things that were fun instead.

He was up early this morning to pursue one of his favourite hedonistic activities: snowboarding. He was taking three girls to Tignes in France where he planned to bed all of them. One at a time, or all together, he really didn't mind. That they were each at least twenty years younger than he didn't bother him either. They were old enough to know how the game was played, so he was paying for the trip and they would foot the bill in a different manner.

He couldn't help smiling to himself as he pictured it.

That was until the little hairs on the back of his neck began to stand up. He was still living in his parents' three-million-pound Georgian house in Higham. Sure, one could argue that he still lived with his mother at forty-seven, but she wouldn't last much longer so soon the house would be his and he could avoid paying inheritance tax because it was his house too.

The Range Rover was part loaded, but the rest of his gear was still in the house, necessitating several more trips back and forth. He cursed himself for being too lazy to pack yesterday. Had he done so, the handyman or the gardener could have been employed to help him load the car. At this time of the day, there was no one else around.

He paused at the rear of the car, squinting into the darkness. Was there someone there? A chill breeze ruffled his hair, what little of it he had left, and he bit his lip in indecision. He opened his mouth to call out, 'Is there someone there?' but realised how clichéd that would sound and so stopped himself.

With a harrumph, he went back to the house, berating himself for being scared of shadows like a child.

Fifty feet away, a shadow detached itself from the pocket of dark in the lee of a tall tree. The shadow was over seven feet tall and appeared taller yet because it wore a top hat, the very top of which was torn so it stuck up at a raked angle. The tall shadowy figure lumbered across the lawn heading for the car but approaching from the front and away from the lights projecting outward from the building.

Moments later the lights came on anyway, the motion sensor triggered by Jason as he struggled out with all the remaining bags, boots, and boards in one load. Something in the dark was creeping him out, so he was going to throw the remaining items on the backseat of the car and get going. The girls were expecting him to collect them soon anyway. He wanted to be on the slopes by early afternoon, and on one of the girls by early evening.

Unable to shift the creepy feeling, he threw his armful through the backdoor as fast as he could and slammed it shut. He didn't care that it was a mess that would most likely tumble out as soon as he opened the door again. He would sort it out after he collected Sophie or, rather, when he collected her as he would need to load her items then.

Without a care that the sudden noise of the rear door slamming would most likely wake his mother, he jumped into the driver's seat and slammed that door too. The engine was already running, chugging away to make the car's interior warm and power his heated seat. Now that he felt much more secure, he stomped on the gas and peeled off down the drive with a slew of gravel.

Fifty feet away, back at the trees, a figure leaned out to watch. No longer concerned he would be spotted and give the game away, the figure, far more normal sized than the first one, started walking after the car. He didn't hurry his pace though: the car wasn't going to get very far.

A snort of laughter escaped Jason's nose as he settled in and wondered what on Earth had got into him. Jumping at shadows at his age? Ridiculous.

The house's long driveway bent around in a big arc to reach the front gate which would automatically open once he got close enough to it. Relaxing, he turned his attention to the stereo. He needed to portray the hip, edgy personality that would lure the girls into his bed. No good listening to Radio Two which was universally considered to be for old people even though he always listened to it when he was alone. As his finger poised over the button to select Crushing Crew Beats volume two, the sensation of being watched returned but in a far more serious way.

Checking his rear-view mirror to see if he were being followed, he found it to be filled with the ghoulish head and face of a giant man. The apparition's pallid skin had the anaemic appearance of a corpse and when he opened his mouth, the sound that came from it was a bone-chilling rasping noise that defied translation.

Jason Pendergrass screamed in fright, an automatic reaction he could not have fought and failed to even try.

Giant hands surged forward, grasping his head on either side as the ghoul came between the front seats to get him.

Across the garden and watching with excitement as he strolled nonchalantly after the Range Rover, the second smaller shadow saw the car swerve and look ready to lose control. For a moment, he worried it might leave the driveway and crash into one of the ornamental displays, of which there were many dotted along the route in and out of the grand house. That wouldn't do at all, so he was thankful to see the car come to a stop to the side of the driveway but still on it.

The victim was in for a real treat, even if he didn't know it yet.

The Ghoul of Christmas Past:
Chapter Two

BREAKFAST

Saturday, December 24th 0900hrs

'There is something screwy here.'

Mary Michaels raised an eyebrow and looked up from her newspaper. She did not agree with conversation over breakfast, she felt it interrupted the flow of her day. Raising her newspaper so it formed a shield in front of her face, she focussed on the article she was reading.

Two fingers looped over the top edge of the newspaper to pull it down. On the other side, her husband, Michael Michaels grinned a cheeky grin at her.

'Good morning, Mary,' he said as if they had not already spoken several times in getting up and starting their day. 'I wonder if perhaps you were too absorbed in what you are reading to have heard me speak?'

'I heard you,' she replied, casting her eyes back to the page.

Michael waited to see if she had anything else to say,

and when it became clear she did not, he persisted. 'I believe I have stumbled across something.'

Mary felt that she had to deal with enough nonsense from her son, Tempest's, shenanigans already. With a sigh, she made eye contact. 'Have you finished your breakfast, dear?'

Michael cocked an eyebrow and looked down at the wreckage of his two boiled eggs with toasted soldiers. 'Yes, dear.'

'Then perhaps you ought to stumble across the kitchen where you will be able to put away the condiments and wash up the dirty plates.' With a flick of her hands, the newspaper once again formed a barrier between them.

Frowning at the Prime Minister's face as it leered out from the front cover of his wife's broadsheet, Michael Michaels tossed a mental coin. Should he push the issue and risk an hour or more of sullen silence as his punishment or withdraw his hypothetical troops from her border? 'There was a theft from the Dickens Museum a few days ago,' he chose to go with full invasion.

With a huff, because she liked to make her feelings abundantly clear, Mary Michaels folded her newspaper, placed it neatly on the table, and fixed her husband with a glare. 'What of it? You told me about it when it happened.'

'Yes, dear, how silly of me to trouble you with conversation.' Her glare intensified. 'You may remember my old Navy buddy, Rob Whittaker. Well, he was talking about the theft the other night in the veteran's bar.'

Mary frowned. 'I do not recall him talking about that.'

'You didn't hear him because you were chatting with the ladies. He said he was the one who reported the theft and that it was mighty strange because the items had been there on his previous pass. When he came back the next time, they were gone, but all the doors and windows were locked. He suggested it was an inside job and had said as much to the police. He'd been called to see the curator of the museum the following day.' He did some mental math. 'That would have been yesterday then. He was expecting a commendation of some kind for his diligence and for handling the situation without feeling the need to phone management et cetera. He also expected they wanted to quiz him about the other guards because if it were an inside job, they might consider him to be the only one they could be sure to trust.'

'Why?'

Michael gave his wife a surprised expression. 'Because he's the one who reported it. If he were also the thief, he'd be a terrible one.'

She nodded, not particularly interested. 'Why are you telling me this?'

Glad she asked the question, Michael got to go back to the original point. 'I mention it now because I note while reading the news myself, that one of the shareholders for the Dickens Museum has gone missing.'

'Missing?' Mary echoed. Then sensing that she had foolishly shown interest, begged, 'So what, Michael? Why are you telling me this?'

'Because that's two things … two crimes in the space of a few days at the same place. Doesn't that feel like it must be connected somehow?' He watched her face for sign that she saw the connection too. When she showed none, he asked, 'Don't you think these things might be connected?'

'A missing person is not a crime,' she replied, lifting her paper once more and opting to be pedantic because it annoyed him when she did. 'Not until a body or a ransom note turns up.'

Michael sniffed in a breath through his nose, breathing deeply and holding it for a second while he squinted his eyes in thought. 'No. There is something screwy about this.'

Now she got it. 'Oh, no.'

'Oh, no?' he repeated her words. 'What oh, no?'

'You're trying to be a detective,' she accused him. 'I knew this would happen. The moment you started getting involved in Tempest's cases, I knew it would come to no good. And I was right, wasn't I?'

Trying not to frown across the breakfast table, Michael nevertheless felt that his wife might be missing the point. 'A man who owns shares in the Dickens Museum has gone missing and things have been stolen from the Dickens Museum.' He remembered something else, adding quickly, 'And let's not forget that Dickens Greatest Works Theme Park just shut with the loss of all jobs. There must be a connection in these things. It stinks like a cover up or a diversion tactic.'

'That's your son talking. That's the exact sort of thing he would say and since he is the private investigator and you are just a retired Royal Navy officer, perhaps you should let him know about it and leave it at that. Besides, the Dickens Museum and Dickens Greatest Works Theme Park are completely different entities, I don't even think they are owned by the same people.'

Michael skewed his lips to one side. 'I don't know. You might be right,' he conceded.

'There you are then,' said his wife, collecting her newspaper again and considering the subject closed.

Generally opting to take the path of least resistance with his wife – it had ensured for a happy marriage thus far - Michael pushed back his chair and began to pick up the crockery and cutlery. 'What's that website Tempest uses to find out about people and companies and stuff?' he asked, taking an armful to the kitchen.

Mary elected to not answer his question, choosing to divert his attention instead. 'We have a few jobs to do today,' she announced. 'I'll need your hand with the groceries, there are books to return to the library, and there's your prescription to collect ...'

His wife's voice faded into the background as he concentrated. There would always be mundane things to do like shopping for lettuce and taking books back to the library. Those tasks could be performed any old time. In the morning, they were driving to Hampshire to spend Christmas with their daughter and her husband and the grandchildren. That was exciting and he looked forward to it. His children and more recently his grandchildren were a blessing. He had to wonder how long it might now take Tempest to produce a child, given how enamoured he appeared to be with his business partner and girlfriend, Amanda.

Thoughts of his children and grandchildren were all very nice but seeing his grandchildren didn't get his pulse racing the same way running around with Tempest did. It wasn't that he was bored exactly, he wasn't looking for an adrenalin rush, at least not consciously. However, the years were creeping on, and a milestone birthday was just around the corner. If he didn't do the things he felt like doing now, soon he might decide he was too old to do them. There might be nothing to the Dickens events, but equally, they could be connected, and it sounded like exactly the sort of thing his son, Tempest, might choose to look into.

'Companies House!' he barked triumphantly when the name suddenly popped into his head. Now all he had to do was work out how to look up the information he wanted.

A face appeared around the doorframe, pinning him to the spot with squinty eyes and a narrow expression.

In his head, Michael Michaels prayed she wouldn't raise her wagging finger. She reserved it for those rare occasions when she wanted to really give him a telling off and he didn't feel it was currently warranted. Granted, he was giving serious consideration to doing just exactly as he felt and had been known to get himself in bother when the mood took him, but the wagging finger only ever led to arguments between them and he didn't want that right before Christmas.

She placed her hands on her hips, which gave her husband reason to make a relieved noise. 'You don't have time to be getting distracted with any nonsense today, Michael,' she warned. 'We are going away in the morning so you need to pack, and we have jobs to do as I have just told you, and, in case you have forgotten, which you probably have, we are going to the theatre this evening.'

'How could I forget that?' he asked, posing a question because then he hadn't actually lied. She'd only been talking about it yesterday, but it had completely slipped his mind again. This was probably due to the fact that he didn't want to go. With Dickens being such a local influence, stage productions of his works were held regularly at different venues. Each Christmas, an open-air performance occurred in the castle grounds which forms a natural bowl. He could agree that the setting was dramatic and impressive, but he would rather volunteer for a rectal exam from a man with hooks for hands while simultaneously retaking his year ten algebra exam than spend three hours trying to stay awake through another Dickens production.

He had no one to blame but himself of course. This year's tickets, much the same as last year's and the year before that were due to foolishly lying about how much he enjoyed it the first time she took him. Had he been truthful and revealed that he would rather spend the evening singing Barry Manilow songs naked at an outdoor piano bar in Siberia, then he would have suffered swiftly but not perpetually.

Mary left him with the dishes as was their custom and went to find her coat, shoes, and handbag. There seemed no escape, but taking out the trash, he sneakily checked over his shoulder and made a phone call.

Grab your copy...
vinci-books.com/ghoul-christmaspast

About the Author

When Steve Higgs wrote his debut novel, *Paranormal Nonsense*, he was a captain in the British Army. He would like to pretend that he had one of those careers that must be blacked out and generally denied by the government, and that he has to change his name and move constantly because he is still on the watch list in several countries. In truth, though, he started out as a mechanic - not like Jason Statham in the film by that name, sneaking around as a hitman, but more like one of those sleazy guys who charges a fortune and keeps your car for a week even though the only thing you went in for was a squeaky door hinge.

At school, he was largely disinterested in all subjects except creative writing, for which he won his first prize at the age of ten. However, calling it the first prize he won suggests that there were other prizes, which is not the case. Awards may yet come, but in the meantime, he enjoys writing mystery and thriller novels and claims to have more than a hundred books forming a restless queue in his mind because they are desperate to be written.

Now retired from the military, he lives in southeast England with a duo of lazy sausage dogs. Surrounded by rolling hills, brooding castles, and vineyards, he doubts he'll ever leave, the beer is just too good.

9 781036 708658